The Gambler's Unwelcome Fall Bride

Cheryl Wright

Copyright

THE GAMBLER'S UNWELCOME FALL BRIDE
(Unwelcome Brides Series – Book Eleven)

Copyright ©2025 by Cheryl Wright

Small Town Romance Publications

Dedication

To Margaret Tanner, my very dear friend and fellow author, for her enduring encouragement and friendship.

To Alan, my husband of over fifty years, who has been a relentless supporter of my writing and dreams for many years.

To You, my wonderful readers, who encourage me to continue writing these stories. It is such a joy knowing so many of you enjoy reading my stories as much as I love writing them for you.

Table of Contents

Chapter One

Eden, Montana – 1880's

"Is there anything else I can get for you, Sir?" Vera Bailey prayed the restaurant customer would refuse any further assistance. Simply looking at him made her cringe. She had no idea what it was about him making her feel so repelled, but she always trusted her instincts.

"That is all," he said, his voice sliding over her like drool from a dog. It took all her strength for Vera to stop herself from shuddering. "I'll have the bill now," he told her.

Vera had felt this way throughout the man's entire stay, as he sat alone at the corner table. Even when she was far away from him.

When he first arrived, his eyes roamed around the room as he walked in the door. He did this for some time before indicating he was ready to be seated. She wasn't sure why, but Vera had the distinct impression the customer had been watching the waitresses, and finally made a decision.

Mary-Ellen was closest to him, and tried to seat him in the middle of the room – her section. He refused, and strode to the corner table where he now sat. The position gave him full view of the dining area. He could see each waitress, as well as the door to the kitchen and the exit. He had been in the restaurant for over an hour now. He'd consumed three courses – vegetable soup, steak with potatoes and beans, and an extra-large slice of apple pie. He also demanded a double serving of cream. Once he'd had his fill of food, the customer ordered a mug of coffee.

There was nothing unusual in any of it, except Vera was convinced he was going to abscond without paying. Why she believed it to be the case, Vera didn't know. She relayed her concerns to the head chef. He glanced at the customer and laughed.

When it came time to pay, she was surprised when the customer opened his wallet. He carried a large amount of cash, and paid for his meal without complaint. "Here's a tip for you," he said as he winked. "Put it in your pocket now. It is only for you and not to be shared."

Vera's heart thudded as her hand came out to take the large bill offered. "Oh!" she said. "It is too much!"

"And yet you are struggling to pay your rent," he said, a sneer on his face.

She suddenly felt light-headed. How did this stranger know about her financial situation? It had to be a lucky guess on his part. She didn't know this man, and wanted nothing to do with him. Would taking his tip, a very large tip, make her obligated in any way? Vera thought not.

The money would cover her food and lodgings for the next four months. She would be a fool to refuse. It was clear he had money. His expensive suit told her so. Not to mention his bulging wallet.

"Thank you, Sir," she said quietly, hoping none of her colleagues heard. "It will make a huge difference."

The man smiled, and that feeling of drool pouring over her surfaced again. She should be feeling grateful to him, not wanting to have a scalding hot bath to remove every breath that came her way.

Vera breathed a sigh of relief as he strolled out the door and onto the street.

It had been a long day and Vera was glad to be going home. Darkness had already descended. She had no choice but to walk through the shadowy streets. She needed to walk down main street to get home before turning onto the alleyway where the boarding house was located. Surely someone would be on Main Street. It would be her saving grace.

Except Vera wasn't convinced anyone would be there this late at night. Regrettably, her survival could hinge on this.

She felt as though she was being watched. What made her feel that way she had no idea. She glanced over her shoulder and saw nothing. She glanced over the other shoulder. Still nothing. Vera stopped walking. Footsteps sounded behind her. Only for seconds, but they were there. There was no doubting it.

She had made this trip hundreds of times before without mishap. This was the route Vera consistently used to return home after each shift. She glanced about. Vera saw no one. She was on her own. So why was she panicking? She ran to the mercantile, she would be safe there she was certain.

Except the mercantile was closed. The door locked. She hammered on the heavy door with her fists. She could see an almost nonexistent stream of light through the glass, but no one came. The family would no doubt be in their private quarters, getting their children ready for bed.

The rapid beating of Vera's heart caused her to feel lightheaded. What should she do? What could she do?

Confusion filled her. Unsure what else to do, Vera grabbed at her skirts. She lifted them and ran. As fast as she could. Faster than she'd ever run before. She stood outside the house where she boarded. She could see the glow from the light in the kitchen. Dear Mrs. Jones always left the light on for her, despite the late times she often had to work. Vera needed to get inside and quickly. Except nobody was around. It was often the case when she worked this late in the evening.

"Mrs. Jones," she called quietly, still trying to make her voice heard without alerting her pursuer.

No one came.

Vera shoved her hand into her reticule. Finding her key proved difficult in her panicked state. What was she to do? Tears slipped down her face. Vera had experienced fear before. But this was far worse than anything she'd ever encountered before. Whoever was after her was still around she could feel it. Feel them. Vera was convinced she could smell them. The air was ripe, and the smell overwhelming.

"It's him," she whispered to the empty air. The obnoxious man in the restaurant. Of this, she was certain. Why he was following her, she may never know.

With her door key finally in her shaking hand, Vera reached for the door — she would soon be inside and out of danger. Before she even got the key in the lock, a hand covered her mouth. His grip was firm, preventing her from screaming and making it hard to breathe. She dropped the keys on the ground. At least someone would know she'd been there, even if they didn't know what happened to her.

Vera kicked, she thrashed about, then, whoever held her, ensured their grip was tight and she couldn't get away. Vera knew then she would never be free again.

Chapter Two

Robinvale, Montana

"You, Sir, are a cheat." Tyler Evans stared the man in the face. The gambler stared back at him, determination written all over his face.

"I did *not* cheat. How dare you!"

Tyler watched as the man reached down; he was certain his opponent was reaching for his gun. Suddenly the man stood, he glared at Tyler. Under the table Tyler's hand hovered over his gun. It had sat on his knee all this time, where it always did during a game. You never knew what another man would do for money.

Jonesy, as he was known, began to lift his hand. Tyler stood, gun in hand. He glared at the other man. The last thing Tyler wanted was a showdown. He had never yet killed a man over a game of poker, and did not want to start now.

Jonesy's surprise was immediately apparent. "Hold on, partner," he said, his voice urgent.

Was the man backing down?

It was at that moment they heard a woman scream. All heads turned toward the sound. It was dark outside; you could barely see a thing despite the moonlight.

"This can wait," Tyler said as he ran for the door. He glanced about outside. There was little to see in the darkness, much to his annoyance. A woman had screamed, there had to be a reason for that.

The moon was high in the sky, perhaps too high. He could barely see a thing. Still, a woman was in trouble – he couldn't stand by and do nothing. His heart hammered as he glanced down the street again. This time he saw something. Movement.

He squinted into the darkness. Glimmers of light were visible in various spots. It was only brief and appeared to be small. He strode toward the flickers of light, carefully, quietly. Finally, he saw what he sought. It was the silhouette of a woman. She was running in his direction. He could now see what was caught by the moonlight—it was her small amount of jewelry.

He hurried toward her as she ran in his direction. She was breathless, and more than a little terrified. As he ran to her, Tyler wondered what had happened. What caused her to scream. Except there was no time now, he had to get her to safety before whoever was after her found the woman with him.

She was now a little more than an arm's length away. He could see the terror on her face and wanted to make it all better. With his gun still in his hand, Tyler glanced about again. He saw no one. He reached for the woman. As he touched her arm, he felt the wet and warmth. She'd been injured. Possibly shot. His heart pounded, and he could only imagine how she was feeling.

Terrified, he was certain. Tyler quickly led her back to his establishment, where she would be safe.

She said nothing but curled herself into him. That told Tyler far more than words could have. He hurried to get her to safety. He pushed her toward the back entrance of his gambling house. It was not necessarily the best thing to do, but being located in the dark alley, they shouldn't be seen. She would be safe there; he'd make sure of it.

The moment she realized he was taking her inside a strange building, she was reluctant to go with him. Not to mention he was unknown to her.

"You're safe with me," he whispered. She didn't answer, but Tyler heard her swallow. He understood her concern. She didn't know him, so why should she trust him?

He opened the heavy door that led into a storage room. Once inside, he locked the door. Something he never did. Once the door was secure, they continued toward the large kitchen.

When the lights hit her eyes, she blinked several times before her eyes adjusted. "Thank you," she said quietly. He could now see she was breathing heavily. How long had she been running?

"I'll guarantee your safety," Tyler told her. He took her through to the kitchen. The chef glanced up. It was not unusual for Tyler to enter the kitchen, and indeed, he did so several times most nights. But never before had he taken a woman, or anyone else for that matter, with him.

"Everything alright, Boss?" his head chef asked. Joey appeared surprised. Tyler knew it was because of the disheveled woman he held onto tightly.

Tyler shook his head, barely moving it. Though it was enough for Joey to understand this was not a time for questions. "I'm looking for somewhere safe to take this lady," he told the chef. Now the man looked confused, but that was alright. He would explain later. But only if he believed it was necessary. The less people who knew the better.

"Pantry."

One word. That's all his chef said, but it was all he needed to say. Tyler looked down into the woman's face. She was petrified. He noticed for the first time she had blood on her face. No, it was on her mouth. And she was ashen, white as a ghost. Her hair was flung every which way. It was clear it had once been perfectly styled. Once again Tyler wondered what happened to her. Whatever had happened, he had to ensure her safety, and that's exactly what he intended to do.

~*~

With the passing of time, Tyler believed it was safe to come out of the pantry. He glanced at the woman, her eyes closed. Was she asleep? He wasn't certain. Tyler didn't want to wake her but needed to get her somewhere safe, somewhere more permanent, comfortable. He touched her shoulder, although he knew he shouldn't. He felt, in this situation, it would be acceptable.

Her eyes fluttered open, then closed again. She was bewildered, he could see it in her expression. "We need to move from here," he said quietly. "I think the immediate danger is passed, but I can't be sure." And he wasn't. Tyler had to decide what to do about her. This stranger who was in imminent danger. He could not leave her to her own devices, because clearly, she could not defend herself.

Not that Tyler expected her to. That was not a woman's job; it was the job of her husband. He looked down at her hands. There was no wedding ring. He should not be surprised, because if she was married, her husband would have looked out for her.

The woman groaned quietly. She lifted her hands, and her fingers went to her lips. Her bloody lips. What had happened to her? Tyler was curious but he was more concerned about getting her to safety. How was he going to do that without having to drag her along with him? It was something he'd been grappling with almost since the moment he brought her here.

"Stay right here," he told her. "I'm going out to check if it is safe for you."

He stood, his legs a little shaky after sitting on the cold hard floor all this time. He could only imagine the woman felt the same. She moved to stand but he shook his head. "I won't be long," he said. "I promise I'll come back shortly. Then we'll talk."

She appeared mortified. Tyler only hoped she opened up to him when he returned. If not, she left him no choice but to hand her over to the sheriff.

Chapter Three

Vera sat on the floor stunned. The stranger left her alone. He said he'd be back shortly, but could she count on that? After all, she had no idea who he was. He could be yet another criminal for all she knew.

As she sat quietly in the pantry, she heard clatter and movement in the kitchen. She remembered being led through that room. It smelled good in there. Far better than the restaurant she worked in, more high-class.

Vera shook her head. She needed to sit here quietly, not have all this nonsense running around in her mind. More likely than not, she was in shock. After what had happened to her, it came as no surprise. She glanced about the room. It was far bigger than she thought it was, perhaps having two people in there made it feel that way. It felt strange now that she was alone again. Empty.

She began to stand, but her legs were full of pins and needles. She clutched a nearby shelf. It helped, but she still couldn't stand easily. The feeling in her legs was uncomfortable. She stomped her feet in an attempt to eliminate the pins and needles. It was then she noticed one of her boots was missing. It must have come off in the shuffle with her kidnapper.

Vera wasn't surprised she hadn't noticed. She was far too busy trying to save herself. She had a terrible taste in her mouth. It was metallic. She had no idea why. She lifted her hand and put it to her mouth. When she pulled it away her hand had blood on it.

At first, she was shocked, but then she remembered. She had gotten away because she had bitten the man. Hard. So hard, his hand had bled and he let her go. He was clearly in pain. He'd even lifted his hand to hit her. Vera seized the chance to escape. She remembered thinking this could be her one and only chance.

She glanced at him for mere seconds, then ran. Trouble was, he was right behind her. That was when she decided to scream. As long and as loud as she possibly could. It was then her rescuer came out into the street and helped her.

She'd glanced back over her shoulder—the kidnapper was gone. Vera could only assume he wasn't willing to fight for her. She felt a wave of relief.

She clutched the shelves again, still trying to get the feeling back in her legs. She wriggled them about, and it helped. Moments later, her rescuer returned.

He stopped where he stood and frowned at her. "What are you doing," he demanded. He was clearly unhappy.

Vera's heart pounded. Not only was she scared, but now she had to deal with this stranger's demands. "My legs..." It was then she found her voice. "My legs had pins and needles. I had to stand up; I had to fix it."

"Are they alright now?" He glanced down at her feet. "Where is your other boot?" He asked, clearly puzzled.

Vera shrugged her shoulders. She too, look down at her feet. "I have no idea," she said firmly. "I must have lost it in the struggle. Far better to have lost a boot than the alternative."

He looked even more puzzled now, more than he did before. "And the alternative being..." He stared at her waiting for an answer. It was an answer she didn't want to supply but knew she must.

"A man, a stranger, he tried... He kidnapped me." It was all she could do not to cry. Not surprisingly Vera was feeling emotional.

He ran a hand over his chin, his eyes pierced hers. "We need to sit down and have a good talk," he said slowly. It was the last thing Vera wanted to do, but she knew it had to be done, if she wanted to be safe.

When she didn't answer, he walked over to her and took her hand. "I will look after you," he said. "On one condition," he continued.

She studied him then, worried what that condition would be. She still didn't answer. Vera was not prepared to commit to something she may not be able to do.

His hands caressed hers. His touch felt good, but Vera knew she couldn't encourage it. Hopefully by now, the stranger had left town, and she was now safe.

"That condition is you stay here in my...establishment" True to form, she still didn't answer. What he must think of her Vera did not know. What she did know was she had to be careful. Very careful. For all she knew, this man, the one who rescued her, was part of the plan to kidnap her.

The pair sat in the man's office. As much as she wanted to feel comfortable in here, Vera did not want to allow herself to be lulled into a situation where she let her guard down. She leaned back against his sofa. It was so comfortable, and she could easily go to sleep here.

Except the man sitting opposite her was asking questions. Correction – he was bombarding her with questions. What happened to her? Who was the man who tried to kidnap her? Had she seen him before? What did he look like? Where did he come from?

Too many questions, she was bewildered. She was unable to answer practically every question this man asked. Finally, he asked one she could answer. "What is your name, and where have you come from?"

"Vera," she said. "Vera Bailey. I live in Eden, where I work at the restaurant. That's where I saw him, or should I say where he saw me." Vera glanced about curiously. "That's not where I am now, is it?" she asked. "The area doesn't look familiar to me at all."

The man frowned. "Not a local then?" As if he realized the stupidity of that question, he shook his head. "I apologize, I didn't mean to say that aloud." He suddenly pushed his hand toward hers. "Tyler Evans," he said firmly. "This, is my establishment." His hands indicated the office and beyond.

Vera wasn't sure what to say, so she said nothing. She offered her hand, since he'd offered his first. His hands were big, hers were tiny in comparison. They were soft too, and gentle. As had happened earlier, his touch did something to her. Vera wasn't sure what that was exactly, but she didn't complain.

"You're in Robinvale," he said cautiously. "You don't know where you are?" He studied her, and it made her very uncomfortable.

"Well, Vera Bailey, what are we going to do with you?" He studied her more closely than he'd done previously. As much as she wanted to fidget under his intense gaze, Vera stiffened and made sure she didn't react.

If this man was going to protect her, Vera was not going to complain. How he intended to do that, she had no idea.

And *that* worried her.

Chapter Four

Tyler sensed there was something strange going on. At first, he thought the woman was hallucinating. But it seemed that was not the case at all. As he continued to study her, he still was unable to fathom what on earth was going on. He'd seen a lot of things in his time, especially as a professional gambler, so Tyler was very surprised at this woman making him so confused.

As he sat behind his desk, he could tell she wanted to get out of here. The room was small, he had to admit, but surely that wasn't the reason.

"What was I thinking?" he asked, then stood. "How long is it since you ate? No, don't answer that. You look... hungry," he said. Tyler shook himself mentally. What a stupid thing to say. How does a person look hungry?

Now he felt foolish. And so he should.

She had a slight smile on her face which was gone almost as it arrived. Clearly, she did not want him to see it. Although he had to admit, it was quite funny when he thought about it. "I don't know," she said as she stared at him. "After I bit him, he put something over my face. I don't remember much after that."

If he hadn't been holding the desk, Tyler may have stumbled. "We need to get you some food, and quickly," he said. Vera stared at him. She now looked confused, but Tyler had no thought of backing down.

She shook her head. "You don't have to feed me," she said firmly. She glanced down then, and again noticed her one boot missing. It seemed to shake her more than anything else had, and Tyler wondered what she was thinking. "What... What did they do to me?" she asked, her voice quiet.

Tyler didn't know how to answer. Because of course, he didn't know what had happened to her. He only hoped it was nothing terrible. He studied her again. She seemed far more stressed than earlier. Perhaps shock was starting to set in, or maybe realization had finally hit her. "It seems they drugged you. Other than that, I don't know." He stared down at the woman, it was clear she was close to tears. It was also obvious she was holding herself together. Tyler wondered how long she could do that, especially given what she'd been through.

His next thought was to get the doctor to check her over. It was a good idea, given the circumstances, but Tyler wasn't certain Vera would accept his suggestion. He walked around the desk to her and reached for her hands. He held them in his own and couldn't help but study her.

"Let's go to the kitchen," Tyler told her. "I have no doubt you should eat something." She seemed fragile and stumbled more than once. He put an arm around her waist to support her. Vera did not complain. Instead, she allowed him to help her. He only hoped she let him keep her safe from the monster who had kidnapped her.

Did she even know the man's intent? Tyler wasn't certain himself, but he had a pretty good idea. He'd heard of this sort of thing before and was convinced he knew who was involved. It worried him. Troubled him greatly. How many other women we're going to end up in this same situation?

Tyler shook the thought away. Right now, he needed to concentrate on caring for this woman. Vera Bailey. She was a long way from home, and someone had to be missing her. If not family, then her work colleagues.

They walked back into the kitchen. It was as though she hadn't been in here before. She glanced about, trying to get her bearings. Her eyes landed on Joey, his head chef, and she seemed to recognize him.

Joey nodded briefly, acknowledging the pair. "What can I get you, Boss?" he asked, keeping his voice low. It was as though he understood her distress.

"Something for the lady," Tyler told him quietly. "She's not eaten for…a while," he said after a brief pause. "And tea." He glanced at Vera. She nodded and he continued. "Tea for the lady, coffee for me." Tyler began to walk away but turned back only moments later. "We'll be in the blue room," he added as an afterthought.

They could get there without passing through the main gambling hall. That way he could keep Vera's presence secret.

As they began the trek up the stairs, Tyler noticed her limping. He glanced down at her feet. Why hadn't he removed her one boot earlier? It again made him wonder what happened the the other one.

"Wait," he said. "Take off your boot, it is hindering your movement."

Vera stopped, stared at him, then glanced down at her feet. She frowned but reached down and removed the boot from her foot. "What... Where is my other boot?" she asked, as though it was the first time she'd notice the anomaly.

It took all his effort not to laugh, although Tyler knew it was no laughing matter. He leaned down, and gently took the dirty boot from her foot. It was then he glanced at her other foot. It was grubby. Not that he was surprised. How long she had been wandering about on the streets in the dark he had no idea. Where she'd been before that, he didn't know, either.

It must have been somewhere here in town, he pondered. Otherwise, she wouldn't have been wandering the way she was. Did that mean her kidnapper was taking her elsewhere when she escaped? As he stood, Tyler gazed into Vera's face. What secrets did this woman hold?

Did she even know? Tyler wasn't convinced. She was dazed and distressed when he found her. Vera stumbled as she'd tried to run, but from whom? That was the real question, and Tyler knew it.

If he couldn't identify her abductor, would saving her be possible? What sort of protector would he be if he was unable to keep that man, or men, away from her?

It was then Tyler knew he would have to get the law involved. As much as he'd like to help her himself, he had little choice. Vera Bailey was obviously in grave danger, and he had to take steps to save her.

Chapter Five

Vera stared down at her feet as she stood on the stairs. With her one boot missing, she couldn't help but wonder where the other one had gone. She glanced up to find Tyler staring into her face. Was he thinking the same thing?

So much had happened to her, but to her dismay, Vera had no idea what that was. In some ways it could be the best thing, because she wasn't certain she wanted to know. He hadn't said, but she had the impression Tyler knew exactly why she'd been kidnapped. She also believed it wasn't for anything good. His expression alone told her so.

"It will all work out, you'll see," Tyler said firmly. It was as though he was trying to convince her everything would be alright. Vera wasn't so easily convinced. "First though let's get you settled. The room I'm taking you to is rarely used, so you won't be disturbed here." He ran a hand across his unshaven chin. Then he frowned. It was clear to Vera he was mulling something over. But what? That was the question.

She didn't want to be kept in the dark. Vera was determined to know what happened to her. "Did you see anyone?" she demanded. He gazed at her. Tyler opened his mouth to speak then close it again. "When you... When you rescued me from that poor excuse of a man," she said, her voice breaking.

This time he was silent for far too long. He shook his head, and didn't say a word. Not then anyway but guided her the rest of the way up the stairs. "This is it," he said. "The blue room as we call it." His hand reached out for the door handle. As he turned it, he faced her. "You won't be disturbed here," he said. "Joey will come up shortly with your food," he added.

Did that mean Tyler was going to leave her alone? Totally by herself in this strange room, in this strange building? The mere thought of it had her heart pounding. As he opened the door, Vera stared at the beauty inside. Everything was of the utmost opulence. How anyone could use this magnificent room, she had no idea. Vera didn't even know what the room was for and couldn't imagine what it would be.

Its beauty was more than anything she'd ever seen before. What she wanted to do now, was run across the room in her bare feet and lay on the exquisite sofa, with its pillows of shades of blue, lined with gold trim.

She stopped herself in time. Vera had no intention of making this room grubby. Her feet, well her one barefoot, was filthy. She glanced down at herself, at her skirts. The hem was covered in dirt and broken leaves. Once more she couldn't help but wonder, where had she been?

Most of all, what Vera really wanted to know was, what had they done to her while she was drugged? That question would haunt her for the rest of her life.

"I..." Vera stared at Tyler for mere moments. "I can't go in there," she said, her voice almost pleading. "The room, it is pristine, and so very beautiful." She looked down at herself, at her crinkled skirts, her dirty feet, and the filth and leaves that clung to the bottom of her skirts.

Tyler stared at her, his expression was one of disbelief. Did he not understand? That a woman of her caliber, her standing in society, as dirty as a street urchin, could not step foot inside that room? Vera shook her head. This time Tyler studied her, his eyes crinkled, and a frown on his face.

"I don't know what you're thinking," he said. "But whatever it is, it doesn't matter. This room is the best place for you to be. No one comes in here, no one." He said the last sentence more firmly than the rest, leaving Vera with little room to argue.

She lifted her dirty foot, letting him see how bad it really was. Instead of the shock she expected, Tyler grinned. "If you thought that was going to put me off," he said with a laugh in his voice and a smile on his face, "you would be wrong."

Now annoyed, Vera put her hands to her hips and stared at him. Tyler didn't budge. Instead, he moved toward her. She watched him cautiously. What was he doing? He was getting closer by the second, and Vera's heart pounded. Without warning, Tyler lifted her. Vera let out a little squeak, so little she was embarrassed about it.

He was grinning again, the scoundrel. Vera wriggled in his arms, but it did nothing. He strolled over to the sofa and dumped her on it. Who did this man think he was? She briefly remembered him saying this was his establishment. But exactly what was that?

He stood nearby watching her, not saying a word but still grinning. She wanted to slap that smile right off his face but did not. He did, after all, save her life. At least that's the way Vera saw it.

"Why did you do that?" she asked. "Surely you understood what I said. I am far too dirty to be in a room such as this."

He grinned again, much to her annoyance. It seemed like this man was one great big annoyance, and he was getting on her nerves. "You didn't leave me much choice," he said. "Your refusal to go in was what caused it. This room," he said waving his arm around to take in the entire large room, "it's barely used, as I said before. It's probably... a year since it was used, perhaps longer. It is the perfect place to keep you safe, to keep you hidden."

His words made Vera feel terrible. Tyler was right, it was her fault that he'd picked her up like a sack of potatoes and dumped her on the sofa. Despite her understanding of this, she was still angry with him. Except, Vera knew she couldn't stay mad for long. She was reminded once again, this man, this Tyler Evans, had saved her life. At least he saved her from whatever that vile man in the restaurant had planned for her.

For that alone, she had to be grateful. And she was.

Vera was far hungrier than she realized. She wiped her lips with the napkin provided, and it made her think of her job back home. Joey, Tyler's chef, had brought a tray with scrambled eggs and toast, and she was grateful for that. As hungry as she was, Vera was convinced she wouldn't be able to eat much, and she was right. As well as a mug of tea, Joey had provided an additional pot of tea. In case she needed it, he told her.

She didn't know them, not really, but Vera had already worked out both Tyler and Joey were kind people. Especially when they'd met only a short time ago. Joey promised to bring something else for her later, not wanting to overload her stomach. He was clearly a good chef.

Vera would have been happy with only a pot of tea. The addition of food was gratefully accepted. What he would bring next, would be a delicious surprise.

"I'm certain I was right" Tyler said. Vera had startled at his words. She'd forgotten he was still in the room, he was so quiet. She stared across at him, curiosity at his words. As if he could read her face, Tyler smiled briefly. "You were hungry," he said. "I was sure you would be. Even while I hoped you weren't."

He didn't say the words, but Vera knew what he meant. *You were starved by your abductor.* His unspoken words cut through her heart. Why anyone would do that she had no idea. But Vera also didn't know why a complete stranger would kidnap her. Someone who had served him well at the restaurant where she worked.

It was now clear to her; he didn't go there to eat. He went there to choose a victim.

Chapter Six

Tyler stared at the reluctant woman sitting on the opulent sofa. She really was quite grubby. If the situation hadn't been so serious, he would probably laugh. Except this was no laughing matter.

He glanced at the dried blood on her arm. The bullet had thankfully only grazed her, and little damage was done. She needed more attention than food and drink, and he knew it. Placing her in this room was wrong. He could see it now, but earlier, all he wanted to do was hide her away.

There were a number of rooms that had the sort of accommodation she required. But only one sprung to mind. It was equally as luxurious as this room but wasn't equipped for gambling like this one.

The Honeymoon Suite.

As much as he was a professional gambler, Tyler would never take a new bride with him to gamble. Sadly, the room in question had been used several times. He always felt bad for the women, since they weren't allowed in the gambling rooms while the games were in progress.

In this case, however, it was perfect. There was a luxurious bathroom, and Vera could soak in the warmth for as long as she wanted. The bed was large and comfortable. Just as well, since he would be sleeping there, too.

Not that Vera would approve, but he couldn't leave her alone. Who knew how desperate her kidnapper was to get her back?

He instinctively knew what this was about. He'd seen it before. Horace Dalton often used his status in society to pluck young women from their workplace or their homes. He would drug them to keep the women compliant, then put them to work in his brothel.

Horace worked in such a way, the law couldn't touch him, and he had always got away with his crimes. Vera was the only woman who had escaped the criminal's clutches. For that, he applauded her, but she wasn't out of the woods yet.

When Joey returned, Tyler would apprise him of his revised plan. Joey was one of the few people who knew of Vera's existence. Nevertheless, Tyler understood he could depend on his loyal staff for support when necessary.

To many, this was a second home.

"What are you thinking?" Vera's voice cut through his thoughts, and Tyler ran a hand across his chin.

"Far more than I'm willing to share," he said quietly. "I should get the doc over here to look at that arm," he said. "Only the less people who know you're here, the better."

Vera glanced down, first at her uninjured arm, then the one with the dried blood. "Oh!" she exclaimed on seeing her bloodied arm. She paled even more than she already was.

Had she forgotten she'd been shot? Tyler supposed it was possible in all the chaos of the past couple of hours. "It's only a graze. Nothing to be worried about," he told her, trying to reassure her.

She nodded briefly, and slight color came back into her face.

Vera was far more vulnerable than Tyler had realized. More than likely, she was still suffering the effects of the drugs Horace had used on her.

The man posed a threat to society and had to be stopped. He used Robinvale as his base, with his main brothel a few miles outside of town. Although he travelled from town to town, picking out new blood for his brothels.

As the women got older and past their prime, he disposed of them. Permanently. Their remains had been found – always miles away from the brothel, ensuring Horace was not implicated. Except the law and everyone else knew he was involved.

Tyler knew he was their killer. The man was brutal, and always had been. Growing up in the same town and attending the same school, Tyler knew Horace Dalton was capable of much more. He could be earning decent money and doing it legally. But Horace had always had an evil streak, and he preferred to do whatever he wanted.

If that included kidnap and murder, so be it. Horace did not blink, or flinch, at the pain he inflicted on innocent woman. He enjoyed it.

Tyler shuddered. The man was pure evil.

"I've decided to move you into a different room," he told her gently. She gazed at him suspiciously. "This one has a bath," he announced. "With running water."

Now she glared at him. He could almost see the cogs of her mind turning over, wondering what he was trying to do. Was Vera wondering if he was in cahoots with Horace Dalton? He needed to put her mind at ease.

"I made you a promise earlier. That you would be safe here. The room you'll be in is large. I'll be able to stay with you much of the time. On the occasions when I can't, I will place one of my security guards outside of your room." He couldn't do more than that.

She nodded but made no comment. Vera had likely been shoved around while she was drugged. Knowing Horace the way he did, Tyler was certain he would have tried to beat her into submission. But not where it showed.

In all likelihood, she would have cuts and bruises where they couldn't be seen. Perhaps even a broken rib or two.

He felt ill at the very thought of it. Tyler was not a violent person, and never had been. In this case, he knew the only way to stop her attacker was to meet violence with violence. Tyler knew the world would be far better off without Horace in it.

Horace's kind of evil was not wanted. Especially here in Robinvale.

~*~

As he opened the door to the Honeymoon Suite, the least used room in the entire building, Tyler watched as Vera's jaw dropped. "This is…" She licked her lips. She seemed lost for words. "It's beautiful," she said, shaking her head. "I can't accept this. I…I have no money," she whispered, her voice almost inaudible.

Tyler studied her. "I'm not charging you," he said, frowning. "It's a gift. From me to you." He could see she still wasn't convinced. "I'll run a hot bath for you," he said, leading her into the luxurious bathroom attached to the massive room.

"I...I can't accept," Vera said. "This is too much." She spun around checking the room out. It was then she spotted her reflection in the full-length mirror. The shock on her face was profound. All color drained away in a matter of seconds.

Tyler quickly guided her from the mirror into the bathroom.

Every possible comfort was included. He was, after all, providing accommodation for his high rollers. Men who had more than enough money to throw away. While they wasted their hard-earned money, their brides were enjoying the extravagance provided by Tyler.

If their wives were happy, those high rollers were happy to spend. Even knowing they might lose it all.

Tyler leaned down and turned on the faucets. "Your bath will be ready shortly," he said. "There are bubbles in the cupboard," he told her, then reached into a cupboard and handed her two large fluffy towels and a face cloth. "You'll find all the toiletries you need in here," he said, indicating low hanging cupboard. "Once you have finished your bath, there will be clean clothes waiting on the bed for you. Toss your current clothes into the trash."

The shocked look on her face told Tyler he'd gone too far. He felt the guilt weighing on him, but knew those clothes were beyond redemption. "There will be a security guard stationed outside your room." He said the words, and as much as he wanted to stay and care for Vera himself, he had much to do. "Enjoy your bath, and soak as long as you like."

He headed out of the room and locked the door behind him.

Chapter Seven

Vera stared at Tyler's back as he hurried out of the room. She glanced down at the luxurious bath he'd arranged for her.

She had never experienced this sort of luxury before. Vera did not come from a rich family – far from it. Her upbringing had been difficult with both parents struggling to make ends meet. Her father had met an early death after an accident on their farm. Mother died not long afterwards; said to be from a broken heart.

The bank reclaimed the family property only a few short weeks later, stating mortgage debt. There was no proof to the contrary. Vera could not get out of that place quick enough. Not that she had much choice.

Moving into town had been the best thing ever. Living in the women's boarding house was even better. Two meals provided every day, as well as lunch for a little extra, if needed. Her own room, where the bed was the most comfortable bed she'd ever slept in.

Losing her parents was heartbreaking, but moving into town turned out to be the best thing for Vera. She found her independence and was no longer living in poverty.

She glanced down at herself. Tyler was right, the clothes she wore were in tatters and filthy. She was filthier than a street urchin, and it made her heart hurt. Vera closed the bathroom door and began to undress.

She stared down into the trash can, and reluctantly tossed her gown into it. It was then she remembered the toiletries Tyler had told her to take as wanted. Vera opened the cupboard he'd indicated and was shocked.

Never in her life had Vera seen so much to choose from. Shampoos, bottles of bath bubbles, soaps, and far more. She reached for the shampoo. Her hair was a mess and needed to be tamed. Lifting the pink bar of soap, she brought it to her face. Breathing in the rose fragrance, it brought a calmness to her. Something she hadn't felt since before she was kidnapped.

Once she had finished undressing, Vera slid into the oversized bath. It felt good. Too good. Vera knew she could spend the rest of the day here. Except her arm stung where the bullet had grazed it.

She was lucky, and grateful. That bullet could have been the end of her. Instead, here she was, in the most opulent room she had ever seen, soaking in the biggest bath she'd ever had the fortune to soak in.

Vera slid down under the water and washed her hair. How she had become so dirty between arriving home from work, which culminated in her kidnap, and now, she had no idea. One thing Vera did know was, whoever that man was, he wouldn't give up easily.

The danger was far from over, and she knew it.

After soaking in the tub for what seemed like forever, the water was going cold. That was a sure sign to Vera she needed to get out. Except she didn't want to. Despite the thought, she pulled out the stopper. She was mesmerized by the swirl of the water as it went down the drain.

More than that, the filth of the water made her feel ill. How had she become so dirty? It made her wonder how she had been transported. The distance between Eden and Robinvale was not short. Under normal circumstances, it would take at least two days. Perhaps longer.

Tears sprang to her eyes thinking about all she'd endured. Even if she didn't recall the details, Vera instinctively knew she had been mistreated. What had she suffered? The bruises on her body told her more than she wanted to know.

At some point in the past few days, she had been beaten. Not where the bruises were visible, but elsewhere. There seemed little point to the exercise if she was unconscious. And since she couldn't recall anything, it certainly seemed to be the case.

Blinking to stop the tears, Vera heard movement in the bedroom. She gasped, then remembered Tyler's words – that clean clothes would be waiting for her when she finished her bath. She stood and wrapped one of the fluffy white towels around herself. Then she took the other towel and secured her hair with it.

Once all the water was gone, she again felt ill. The base of the bath was covered with grime. She turned the faucet on and ushered out all the dirt with the flow of hot water.

Vera stood in the bath, wrapped in the towel. She didn't know how long she stood there, but the click of the door closing pushed her into action. Vera gingerly opened the door that led into the bedroom.

There on the bed lay a set of clothes worthy of a lady of wealth. Vera was far from that and felt unworthy to wear the gown that lay perfectly flat on the bed. Except she had no choice.

Next to the gown was a complete set of undergarments. Her now clean fingers ran over them. The fabric was the softest she had ever felt.

Vera dressed quickly, unsure if Tyler would let himself into the room when he returned or wait to be invited. To her surprise, everything fitted perfectly. She wasn't certain how Tyler had got it so right, but he had. No matter, she was truly grateful.

Once fully dressed, she walked over to the window and sat in the comfortable chair there. She watched out the window, keeping far enough back so she couldn't be seen.

Vera was startled at the tap on the door. "Come in," she called, not really thinking about the danger. Likely, because there was security outside the door.

The door handle turned, and Tyler stepped inside. He grinned as he approached. "You look much better. I hope you feel refreshed." He walked across to where she sat. "Good, the clothes seem to fit?"

"They do. Perfectly," Vera said. "Thank you for arranging all of this. I do appreciate it, even if I didn't say so earlier."

Tyler held a small paper bag, and seemed to suddenly remember it was there. "This is for you," he said as he passed it over. "I'll arrange for more clothes now I know the sizing is correct."

Vera didn't know what to say. Tyler was being extremely generous. Far more than she would have expected from a stranger. "How can I ever repay you?" she asked.

Tyler kept silent for mere seconds before answering. "I don't expect you too," he said firmly. "If one of my sisters was in this same situation, I'd like to hope someone would look after her." He sat on the chair opposite her. "Aren't you going to open your gift?" His eyes went to the bag in her hands.

Vera had already forgotten about it. The drugs she was given must be messing with her brain. She was having trouble focusing. Vera glanced down into the bag and pulled out the hairbrush. "Thank you," she said, noting it was yet another thing Tyler had done to help her. Vera wondered if he was connected to the man who kidnapped her. Was he getting her to like him to ensure Vera obeyed whatever he demanded?

She shook herself mentally. From the contact she'd already had with him, Tyler was not like that. He was a nice man, one intent on looking out for her.

At least she hoped he was. Otherwise, she was in a bucket load of trouble.

Chapter Eight

Tyler watched as Vera stared down into the bag. Had he not known the circumstances, he would think she had not seen a hairbrush before. It was a simple item, something every woman needed. At least that's what his sisters always told him.

Watching her now, Tyler realized how truly awful this situation had become for Vera. Once again it made him wonder how long she had been held captive. With her mind in a blur, it was something they may never know.

Vera removed the brush from the bag and stared at it. If he didn't know better, you would think he'd given her a diamond bracelet. She looked at that brush as if it was priceless. In a way he guessed it was.

"Thank you," she said quietly. She glanced up at him then, her slate gray eyes studying him. Her eyes were sad, not that Tyler could blame her. Her entire life had been ripped away. All due to the selfishness of one man. That man, Horace Dalton, had done this before. Except on those occasions, Tyler was not in a position to save the victims.

It still cut him to the core. Knowing someone he'd grown up with was capable of such evil. What led Horace down this path, Tyler would never know. What he did know, was that his childhood friend needed to be stopped.

Vera still held the brush in her hand, rotating it, looking it over. Her hair was still wet and was dripping down over her shoulder. She looked so vulnerable, he wanted to reach out and hold her. Except Tyler knew he couldn't do that. Even though it was clear Vera needed comforting.

"You really didn't need to do this," she said, this time her voice was firm. Unlike the last time when she sounded very unsure. "I won't be here long," she said as she glanced up at him again. Tyler knew he had to be vigilant. Her eyes drew him in like a fish on a line. In them, he saw her vulnerability. Now and then, her true self appeared. Once the drugs were out of her system, perhaps he would see the real Vera Bailey.

She continued to stare into his face, and he felt like an insect under glass. How she did that, he did not know. It took all his strength not to squirm under her gaze. "Neither of us know how long you'll be here." He stared into her face; her eyes were like the window to the world. Every time he glanced at them, it hit him in the heart. He wasn't sure what it was about, but knew it meant he felt something for her.

He hoped that something wasn't pity.

"I... You know who did this?" she asked quietly.

It was clear Vera wasn't certain about this, but he had no intentions of lying to her. "Perhaps." She stared at him so hard, Tyler was certain his heart would shatter. "I believe it to be someone I grew up with," he said, his eyes never leaving her face. Until he could no longer take it. Why he felt the full impact of the guilt that belonged to Horace, Tyler didn't know.

Except he did.

He could have taken Horace down more than two decades ago – in their teenage years. In that instance, it wasn't a kidnapping, not in the true sense. The person he had previously thought of as his friend, had dragged a teenage girl behind the school shed. That memory had never left Tyler. The girl crying and screaming did not deter Horace. Her skirts forced up around her waist, Horace was about to do his worst.

Tyler's hand hovered over his gun; the memory of that moment was still so vivid. In hindsight, knowing now what Horace had almost done back then, instead of merely striking the man, Tyler should have dropped him where he stood. Had he done so, Vera and many other women would not have to endure the pain Horace inflicted on them.

Except for the rest of his life, Tyler would have to live with the knowledge he'd killed a man.

Tyler had broken all ties with Horace Dalton. To this day, Horace had not learned from the experience, nor had he changed. Not even slightly. In a small town like Robinvale, word got around. He often heard about the terrible things Horace had done. Of the women he had kidnapped, drugged, and installed in his brothel – all against their will.

The mere thought of it made him sick to his stomach. If he ever saw Horace Dalton again, Tyler feared he would kill the man in cold blood. After seeing firsthand for himself what Horace was capable of, it made him even more determined.

 As much as he wanted to stay, Tyler knew he needed to leave. The more time he spent with Vera the more endearing she became to him. It was not what Tyler wanted. He was an independent man, not relying on anyone for anything. He certainly wasn't going to start now. "I must go," he said as he stood.

Vera glanced up at him, her eyes sad. He felt guilty but had to leave. Tyler had things to arrange. He had to ensure Vera's safety. There was already a guard at the door. No one could get in. They would not get past his guard. The man was used to breaking up fights, tossing out cheats, and keeping the peace.

She said nothing at his statement. Didn't complain, and didn't whine. He expected at least one of those, but it didn't happen. "I'll be back as soon as I can," he told her as he headed for the door. "Make yourself comfortable, take a nap if you want. You are your own boss, make the most of it."

Moments later, Tyler was standing outside the door. His trusted guard stood like a soldier. He acknowledged Tyler with a nod that was barely noticeable. He had a gun on each side of his hip. Tyler hoped and prayed they would not be necessary.

He near ran down the stairs, his eyes alert for any trouble. He would speak to the sheriff and do whatever he could to keep Vera Bailey safe.

At the bottom of the stairs, Tyler took a moment to steady his breathing. He was anxious to ensure Vera's safety. After allowing himself a few minutes to recover, he strolled purposely to the door. He stood inside momentarily, then opened the door and glanced about. There was nothing to see out there, which was reassuring.

He stood there, like a sentinel, and waited, hoping Horace Dalton showed himself. Tyler's hand hovered over his holster. The action made his heart race. He had wanted to eliminate the man for many years but had no proof of what he had done.

Now Tyler had the proof he needed but knew it didn't justify killing Horace in cold blood. Besides, that wasn't the way he worked.

Movement across the road and a few doors up caught his eye. Tyler stiffened. And his hand reached for his gun—despite his principles.

He would do just about anything for Vera. She was incredibly vulnerable and needed his help. But what good would he be to her if he was in jail? Tyler knew he would be useless and could no longer protect the woman he had saved.

It simply would not do. He glanced across to his left as movement caught his eye again. This time it was someone he wanted to see. The sheriff was coming his way and waved to Tyler. "Howdy," Sheriff Peter Jones said. "You look like someone with a problem", he added, then sat down on the wooden bench nearby.

"I was checking the coast was clear," Tyler said, his eyes burning into the sheriff's. "Horace Dalton has been at it again. Except his latest victim escaped." He sighed. How many more times would this go on? Tyler hated to even think about it. Horace had been committing his awful deeds for many years, but he was still escaping the consequences.

Tyler vowed there and then he would not allow Horace to continue the way he'd been going. If that meant he ended up in jail, so be it. It wasn't something he wanted to think about, but women's lives were at risk.

Feeling as though he was caught in a fishing net, Tyler sat down with the sheriff. As he spoke, telling the sheriff about Vera's experience, he couldn't help but see the worry on Peter Jones' face.

It was clear to Tyler the sheriff also wanted this to end.

"We must do something this time," Peter said. "And now we have the proof. She is upstairs in your best room?"

As much as the sheriff sounded positive, Tyler wasn't convinced this was the time they would get Horace Dalton. The man was as sly as they came. He'd gotten away with his crimes so many times now, why would this time be any different?

Chapter Nine

Vera awoke, unsure about where she was. She glanced about the room. She knew she wasn't at home because this room was far too luxurious. Where was she? That was the question. She pulled herself up and sat nervously on the edge of the bed.

Her mind was still in a fog. She seemed to remember a man helping her. But for what reason? Vera looked down at her clothes. She tensed—these clothes did not belong to her. Nothing made sense.

A tap at the door startled her. "It's me, Tyler." The voice was familiar, but Vera couldn't place him.

Should she invite him in? Is that what the man wanted? Tyler. "Come... Come in," she said quietly. The tap came again at the door. Perhaps he hadn't heard her. Vera's heart raced as she headed toward the door. She opened it, but only slightly.

Not that it would matter, if somebody wanted to force their way in, they would do it. The second she opened the door and saw Tyler standing there, her memories of him flooded back. Her heart fluttered, but Vera had no idea why.

Perhaps it was because she'd remembered something about him. He'd helped her. After she was kidnapped. How many drugs had been pumped into her? Apparently, it was a lot, since her mind was still a fog. She stared at the man standing next to Tyler. He was a stranger. And it bothered her.

"Are you alright?" Tyler asked her as he frowned.

Clearly, she wasn't—the last days were a blur. There was so little she remembered about what happened. She shook her head, then backed off and went to the chair by the window. The two men followed her. Vera's heart pounded. She needed to sit down as she now felt lightheaded. This was all too much, but she had no idea how to make it all stop.

Her greatest fear was that nothing would make it stop, that Horace Dalton would come after her again.

Vera gasped. Moments ago, she could not think what had happened to her. Now, it all flashed in her mind. It was despite the fact she'd been drugged. Her hands in her lap as she sat, Vera didn't ask for introductions, and she didn't invite anyone to sit down. And yet, the stranger, who turned out to be the sheriff, sat in the empty chair opposite.

"Miss Bailey," the sheriff said gently. "I am Sheriff Peter Jones. Tyler has explained your, uh, situation.

We have been trying to stop this man for decades. With your help, we can finally do so."

Vera studied the sheriff. "That's all and good," she said. "But how am I supposed to do that? I can barely remember what happened an hour ago," she told the sheriff firmly. "I... I didn't even recognize Tyler to begin with." He looked at her strangely, as though he didn't understand what she meant. "When I opened the door," she said. "I had no idea who he was, but then it came flooding back to me. I don't know how I'm supposed to help you when my mind is in a whirl."

Vera thought she was on the verge of a breakdown. How could this be happening to her? She studied the sheriff for mere minutes. Suddenly he frowned. He then reached out and covered her hand.

"I rarely promise anything, especially to victims of crime," he said. "I've been after Horace Dalton for decades. I'm tired of chasing him and getting nowhere. This time..." He wiped a hand across his forehead. Vera could still see beads of sweat there. "This time, I'm going to get him. And that's a promise."

She glanced across at Tyler. He seemed as shocked as she was. The sheriff stood. "If I'm going to do this, I need to get started." He hurried to the door, pulling it open quickly and leaving with the same level of haste.

Tyler glanced down at her, then sat in the vacated chair. She watched his every move and waited for him to tell her what he thought of the sheriff's statement. Except Tyler seemed to be in a daze, just as Vera was.

She leaned forward, then covered his hand. Tyler glanced up at her, his eyes questioning. He shook his head, then spoke quietly. "I don't know what to tell you," he said, his words coming out forcefully.

"Then don't," Vera said. "Don't say anything if it's not true."

Tyler stood then, clearly ready to leave her alone. "I'll arrange a tray of food for you," he said.

Vera was not hungry, not really. Even so she did not refuse him. "I appreciate it," she said quietly, then stared out the window. Vera wondered if Horace Dalton was still searching for her. He obviously would not be pleased she escaped, hence the gunshot wound she had on her arm. She'd been lucky, but many women were not.

Vera did not know how she escaped. Had no recollection of it at all. No matter how it happened, she was grateful to be here. Safely tucked away from the danger lurking outside.

Thanks to Tyler Evans, she was alive. But how long could she stay here? She didn't want to infringe on his life, although Tyler didn't seem to be bothered.

He was a good person, anyone could see that. He'd gone to great lengths to ensure her safety, but how much longer could she hide here? It made Vera wonder if her being here infringed on his business. It was the last thing Vera wanted.

Without Tyler she would probably be lying dead in the street. And the alternative? She would likely be a soiled dove, doing the last thing she ever wanted to do.

~*~

Vera awoke at the tap on the door. She had no idea how long she had been sleeping.

"It's me, Joey. Can I come in?" She recognized Joey's voice, the chef she'd met downstairs and again when he brought her a tray of food earlier. Although she hadn't eaten a lot it was clear he was a talented chef.

Vera called for him to enter. Moments later the door opened, and Joey stepped inside. He strode over to her and placed the tray on a side table. "Nothing heavy," he said. "I made you chicken pot pie. If you can't eat it or don't like it, don't worry. You've been through a lot. Which can upset your appetite." He lifted a mug of tea from the tray, and Vera was elated.

She reached for the tea, then took a sip. Vera sank back into the chair. Tea always calmed her nerves.

Joey stood there looking down at her, a worried look on his face. "You are going to eat something aren't you?"

"I... I will, I promise." Never had anyone worried about her as much as Joey and Tyler did. It was a totally new experience for Vera. She knew it was a good thing, but it also made her feel uncomfortable. What if she was putting their lives in danger, simply by helping her?

Joey turned away and headed for the door. "Thank you," she called after him. It was an afterthought, and that made her feel terrible. Both men were doing what they could to help her, and she barely acknowledged their efforts.

Vera knew she had to do better. If only for her own peace of mind.

Chapter Ten

Tyler stood inside the building. He pulled the window covering aside and looked out. There was nothing to see, much to his annoyance. He was looking for Horace Dalton. What he wanted to do to that man should not even be thought about.

The same things Horace did to women should be done to him. Drugged, tied up, and dumped somewhere he had no idea about.

Within seconds of the thought hitting him, Tyler knew it was wrong. Believing it was wrong, however, didn't stop him from wanting to carry it out. Except Tyler knew he would never do so – it wasn't in his nature.

He felt someone come up behind him before he confirmed anyone was there. He spun around, almost losing his balance. His hand went to his gun, which shocked even Tyler.

"Settle down, my friend." Joey was right. He needed to take a breath. He was hot and bothered over all this business with Vera. Not that it was her fault, far from it. Horace Dalton—the man roiled him without even being in his line of view. Joey put a friendly hand to his shoulder. "You can't help Vera in this state. Take the time to reassess and calm yourself." Tyler glanced at him, but didn't answer.

"Follow me to the kitchen." Joey did not make a request, it was a demand, although Tyler was the boss, his chef often bossed him around. "I won't take no for an answer," Joey told him.

Tyler knew he was right, he hadn't eaten for most of the day. His concern for Vera was fluid. He knew exactly what Horace Dalton was capable of. Sheriff Peter Jones knew, too. The three men had grown up together. They'd all gone to the same school, lived in the same town, and knew the same people.

How could this be, that two of the three men were upstanding citizens, and the other was a vicious criminal? It was a question Tyler often asked himself. He knew he would never have an answer. He said nothing but followed Joey into his kitchen. It always felt cozy in here, with the various aromas permeating the air. Joey had been with him for several years, and Tyler hoped he would be here for a long time to come. "It smells good in here," Tyler said. Then he shook his head. Joey stared at him.

"Sit yourself down," Joey said. "What is your poison? I have chicken pot pie freshly out of the oven, or there's steak. If neither of those work, I can rustle something else up for you."

Tyler felt defeated. Perhaps if he ate something he might be able to think better. He heard the door at the back of the kitchen rattle His heart pounded. Had Horace found Vera? "It's Peter, open the damn door," the sheriff yelled as he continued to pound on the door.

Joey raised his eyebrows and grinned. "I think you better let him in," he said.

Tyler stood, his gaze going toward the door that was normally unlocked. He glanced through the small glass panel on the door, and was able to confirm it was indeed Peter Jones. He quickly unlocked the door and let the sheriff in.

"Since when did you lock this door?" Peter demanded. "In all the years you've had this... business," he said, "I have never known you to lock this door." He glared at Tyler then.

Tyler took a step back. He closed and locked the door behind him. "Since I was harboring a woman targeted by that miserable excuse for a man." Peter knew exactly who he was talking about, and did not dispute Tyler's words.

"I plan to arrest Dalton and lock him in the cells. I would rather that was sooner than later," Peter said. "All we have to do now is secure him."

Tyler knew the sheriff was right. The hardest part was going to be catching Horace. He had years of practice, keeping away from the law. He moved all over the country looking for new blood, new women.

As if that wasn't bad enough, he disposed of the ones he had enough of. Those who had outlived their usefulness. Those, who in Horace's eyes, were now too old, were eliminated. Of course, the profits never went to the women, they were essentially slaves.

Horace only occasionally came back home to Robinvale. And when he did, he kept a very low profile. It was as though he knew if he showed his face, the sheriff would arrest him.

Until now there wasn't a lot of evidence against him. The women working for him refused to give evidence. Everyone knew it was because he threatened them. None of his soiled doves were local. That meant they had no family to help them out of the situation they found themselves in, through no fault of their own.

Just as he'd done in Vera's case, Horace travelled from town to town, finding his next victim.

Tyler shook his head. The entire scenario made him sick to his stomach. "We've tried so many times before," Tyler told the sheriff. Not being able to catch the mongrel was disheartening. Once again, his mind went to the gun in his holster.

Anger built up inside him every time Tyler thought about Horace Dalton. How he ever allowed that man to be his friend, Tyler didn't know. He was sure Peter Jones felt the same way. "Come and sit down," Joey said. "I was just getting a meal for Tyler, what can I get for you, Sheriff?"

"That's mighty kind of you. Whatever you have works for me." The sheriff breathed in the aroma of the kitchen. "It sure smells good in here. I could take this all day."

Tyler knew exactly what he meant. Not only did the aroma get to him, but Joey was a good man. And an excellent chef. He could whip up a meal in a matter of minutes. Not only that but it would be the most delicious meal a man had eaten for some time.

When Tyler first took over the hotel, he'd planned it would be just that—a hotel with rooms for rent. Things changed along the way. He frequently had requests from guests about where they could gamble. There was nowhere in Robinvale they could do that. As the demands mounted, he saw the potential, and Tyler etched out a plan.

He had several of the rooms gutted and converted to places designed for gambling instead of accommodation. Each room had a small bar along with a privy. That way his guests did not need to leave the room to attend to their personal requirements. Or quench their thirst.

As a result of his meticulous planning, business picked up substantially. Gamblers came from everywhere, not only the county, but all parts of the country. It was the best thing he could have done.

Being a gambler himself, Tyler enjoyed his new business. And it was profitable for him. He didn't consider himself a high roller, but he was good at what he did. One thing he did not allow was cheating. Jonesy was lucky—had Tyler not needed to rescue Vera, there would have been serious consequences to his cheating. Instead, the man got to walk out of the door unharmed.

It was the first time Tyler had detected a cheat in his gambling house. He hoped it would be the last. Right now, he did not have the time for that sort of drivel. Not only did Vera need his protection, but he also needed to locate Horace Dalton.

Hopefully this time he was either arrested or eliminated. Either one was fine by Tyler.

Chapter Eleven

At first, Vera only drank the tea. She glanced at the food Joey had brought for her. It looked good. Really good. She leaned forward and inhaled. Her stomach rumbled. Did that mean she was hungry and didn't realize it?

She picked up the knife and fork. Vera cut a small piece of the chicken pot pie. Steam rushed out of the pastry. Now she was able to get an even better aroma of this wonderful dish. It was easy to tell Joey was a good man. He had done everything he could to ensure she ate.

Vera still wasn't sure where she was. She knew she was in Robinvale, which was in Montana, but that was all she knew. It seemed to be a fair distance from her home in Eden. That alone told her a lot. She had been transported from her home all the way here in the cold of the night. It might be fall, but the evenings were still quite cool. Had she been appropriately protected from the cold?

Vera shook herself mentally. She needed to stop worrying about what was past. She couldn't change what had happened, but she could change the future. With Tyler's help that was. It was crystal clear she could not do this alone. She also could not allow Horace Dalton to get away with her abduction.

The man was a menace to society. Particularly when it came to women. What right did he have to snatch women off the street? To turn them into sex slaves for money? The mere thought of what could have happened to her roiled Vera's stomach. She stared down at the food on the plate again. She wanted to eat it she really did, but now she felt ill.

Her mind was her problem right now. She had to try and forget what had happened, forget what may have happened. Was she violated in any way? Tears sprung to Vera's eyes. It wasn't the first time she'd thought this way, but it was the first time she thought it may be true.

Her stomach rumbled again. Proof she needed to eat. Vera lifted her fork again, placing a small amount of food in her mouth. She closed her eyes. It was so good, better than she'd had in a long time. Whether that was because she hadn't eaten for goodness knew how long, she didn't know.

Tyler had told her Joey was a great chef. Vera knew it was an understatement. Before she realized, Vera had eaten almost everything on her plate. She took another sip of tea and leaned back against the comfortable chair.

She could certainly get used to this. But she also wanted to go home, except home was no longer safe.

~*~

Vera was startled by the knock at the door. How long had she been asleep? The door slowly opened, and she turned to see who was there. She was greeted by Tyler, and also the sheriff.

She was tired. Was she expected to answer questions again? Vera didn't know why she was so tired, except maybe it was the stress of the situation.

Tyler stared at her, then his gaze went to her arm. "You're bleeding again," he said.

Vera followed his line of sight. Tyler was right she was bleeding, but it wasn't much. She shrugged her shoulders. "I'm sure it's nothing to worry about," she told him.

He studied her closely, as did the sheriff. "How did that happen?" the sheriff demanded. He seemed none too happy, but Vera knew her answer would not appease him.

"Horace did it," Tyler snarled. "Luckily it was only grazed. It could have been far worse."

"Regardless of the result," Sheriff Jones said, "his intent was far worse. That is enough for me to arrest him."

"We have to find him first," Tyler said. His gaze pierced the sheriff, and Vera felt as though she was watching some sort of standoff. She probably was.

Sheriff Jones ran a hand across his chin. "This time is the last time. Horace Dalton has had far too much time out of jail." He shook his head. "This time is the last time," he repeated, his words far more assertive this time.

Tyler gazed at him. Vera did the same. Was sheriff Peter Jones making another promise? Because that's exactly what it felt like.

"You can't guarantee that," Vera said. "It seems that evil man has got away with this for many years. Why should this time be any different?"

"Because this time we have a witness." Sheriff Jones stared at her. It was clear he meant Vera. His words shook her to the core. She had been through so much already, and didn't want to go through anymore.

Tyler gazed at her. He stepped toward her until he was close enough to put an arm around her shoulders. "I'll be here with you," he said quietly. "You won't go through this alone. That I can promise."

Vera shuddered. It was clear the only way Horace Dalton would be caught and jailed was through her. Vera's evidence. She wanted to help, she really did, except she wasn't certain she could go through it. Tell her story all over again. Already she'd done it so many times, and she was weary.

Tyler glanced down at her, his eyes assessing. "I know it will be challenging," he said. "I will be there every step of the way," he told her gently. The more time she spent with this man, the more she liked him. She even felt attuned to him. Vera wasn't sure why.

She glanced from one man to the other, took a deep breath, then closed her eyes momentarily.

"We will both be there with you every step of the way," Sheriff Jones told her.

Tyler studied her, his eyes searching her face. He was trying to fathom what she was thinking. Vera rarely let people in. She wasn't about to start today. "I don't think I can," Vera said softly. She glanced from one man to the other, knowing fully they relied on her to put Horace Dalton away for good. "I'm not that strong. People think I am," she said, her eyes piercing the sheriff. He was the one asking, so he was the one she targeted with her gaze.

The sheriff licked his lips then turned to face Tyler, who shook his head gently. It was as though he was going to let her off. Vera felt relief at what she believed. "This man," Peter Jones said firmly, "has terrorized women for more than two decades. *You*, *and only you,* have the power to put him away forever."

The sheriff then turned and strode across the room to the door. As he held the handle, he turned back and looked at her. She could see the sadness in his face. There was no sign of contempt or any sort of hatred for her not doing what he wanted.

Sheriff Peter Jones was not a forceful man. He was a man who understood her fears. Her biggest fear, Vera had to acknowledge, was Horace Dalton snatching her again.

Chapter Twelve

Tyler's gaze went from the sheriff to Vera. He'd known Peter Jones so long, not once had he seen this expression he now held on his face. Peter was determined to put Horace away for good, Except, he couldn't do it without Vera's cooperation.

There was only one thing for it, he had to somehow convince Vera to give evidence in any trial that resulted. She would not be put at risk; he wouldn't allow that. Peter wouldn't want it anyway and would not contemplate such a thing.

His arm was still around her shoulder. It felt comfortable, and he was in no hurry to move it. He stared down into her face and Vera gazed into his eyes. Tyler didn't know what was happening to him. This feeling he had in the pit of his stomach, and in his heart, they were different to anything he'd ever felt before.

Of course, he'd never given refuge to someone running for their life before. Tyler had answered his own question before he'd asked it. He felt something, why would he not? He had saved a woman from certain death. Now that he thought about it, it was unlike Horace to shoot one of his victims. Not a new one anyway, he needed to get what he needed from them first.

There was only one explanation Tyler could come up with. Vera was strong willed. Horace didn't like that. Perhaps he decided it was easier to get rid of her than try and force her to comply.

So why did she refuse to help convict the man? Was she afraid he was going to come after her again? It was impossible. She would be surrounded by not only the sheriff and his deputies, but also Tyler. He trusted no one else when it came to Vera's safety.

He mentally shook himself. He trusted Peter, and that would never change. He was one of the few people Tyler had confidence in. After all these years, he knew Peter Jones better than anybody else in this town.

Tyler totally understood why Vera was reluctant. He had no idea how he could change her mind. Instead of trying to convince her, he led her over to the window. There he guided her into the chair where she seemed to feel the most comfortable.

In all this time of Tyler's contemplation of the situation, Vera said not a word. He sat in the chair opposite her and stared out the window. It was so peaceful out there and he could see why she liked to do this. He didn't bombard her with his reasons for helping the sheriff with the Horace Dalton case, but instead, he remained silent.

Neither one of them said anything for some time. It wasn't until there was a tap on the door, Tyler moved. He suddenly stood and headed toward the door. He was concerned that Horace would find out where Vera was hidden. But this wasn't Horace, that much was clear.

Horace would have not knocked on the door, he would not even pound at the door. He would have killed the guard outside and shot his way in. It was unfortunate but that was the way it was with Horace. It didn't matter what he did, violence of some sort was always involved.

Tyler gingerly opened the door, but only slightly. Joey stood on the other side, his smile brightening Tyler's dark mood. "I've come for the dishes," he said cheerfully. Then his voice was lowered. "I hope Vera ate something this time," he said. Joey looked past him into the room. Vera still sat in the chair watching out the window. "Aren't you worried about her? Sitting in that chair, staring out that window all the time. She seems to do little else."

Joey was right, except Tyler didn't know what he could do about it. There wasn't much Vera could do except hang out in this room and watch out the window. Unless of course he found something useful for her to do. He glanced at Joey and wondered if he needed help in the kitchen. Although he didn't voice his thoughts. Instead, he would mull it over in his mind for a while.

Doing that would give him time to think up other things he could get Vera to do. She was safe here, not only in this room, but anywhere in this building. Gambling was a volatile game. It meant Tyler had a number of security guards around the place.

He would talk to her, find out what she enjoyed doing most. Provided she was away from the public eye, there was a lot open for her to do. Why he didn't realize how bored she was, Tyler would never know. Except his focus was on her safety, not keeping her entertained.

"How safe would that be?" Vera seemed surprised at his question. "I… it would be good, I should be busy. I am truly bored sitting in here all day."

Tyler studied her. Vera did not look scared. She didn't seem at all worried, which was confusing. Although he had explained she would be safe here. He had a number of armed guards, which meant no one would get in without detection. Perhaps she understood. "I'm sure there's a lot you can do here, to keep you busy. Can you cook?"

Vera stared at him in amazement. "And Joey is alright with this?"

It seemed like a rhetorical question to Tyler, but he answered her anyway. "It was his suggestion. He was worried about you being bored, sitting there all day, looking out the window. He was right to say so." Tyler was so focused on keeping her safe, he thought about nothing else.

"Yes, I can cook, of course I can. I'm not a chef, far from it. I'm certain though, Joey would not need someone who's a chef." Her words were snappy. Vera sounded at the end of her tether. Not that Tyler could blame her.

Somehow, he needed to smooth over his awkward questions. "You're right, of course you are. Joey is alone in that kitchen. I don't know why I've never given him an assistant. It gets quite busy in there when there are games on." The moment he said the words, Tyler wanted to take them back.

He hadn't taken the time to explain to Vera what he did. Was he ashamed of how he made money? He didn't think so. Then why had he not told her? "Work here is periodic," he told her, his eyes seeking anything but her face. He suddenly felt ashamed of his life's work. Which made no sense, as it made people happy. Except perhaps, when they lost a lot of money.

Gamblers came here of their own free will. No one forced them or enticed them. Some of them stayed here in the luxurious accommodation, others chose to stay at the saloon. Those who did the latter, were not serious gamblers. They were travelers who just wanted a bit of fun. The serious ones were prepared to pay big money. It was those men Tyler gave near-free accommodation.

"If you feel up to it, I can take you downstairs to the kitchen now." This time he sought her face. Instead of being shrouded with sadness, she now appeared delighted.

Vera stood. She brushed down her skirts, as if trying to remove the wrinkles. It was then Tyler realized, he needed to procure more clothes for her. There was probably much more Vera needed, but how could he get them without people asking questions?

It was a question he needed to ponder. In the meantime, he would deliver her to Joey. His chef would keep her safe.

Chapter Thirteen

Excitement ran through Vera.

She only hoped Joey had plenty for her to do. As Tyler took her down the stairs, he held her hand. Did he think she would run away? It was not something she would even contemplate, not with a killer after her. After all, Horace had tried to kill her once before.

"I don't know why I've never suggested a helper to Joey. And he's never asked for one before." Tyler glanced at her briefly as he spoke. Was he trying to convince her of something? It took almost nothing for Vera to agree to working in the kitchen. Boredom was not something she liked. For some reason Tyler had assumed she enjoyed staring out the window for hours on end.

There was nothing to see out there. A few houses and some stores. Plus, a handful of people on the street. Mostly what she did, was ensure Horace Dalton wasn't out there. The fact she couldn't see him didn't mean he wasn't there.

"You're certain it's safe? Horace can't get in?" It was her biggest fear. Never before in her life did she endure the fear of being so afraid. Living in Eden, there was nothing to be fearful of. Until Horace Dalton came to town.

It made Vera wonder if anyone had noticed her missing. Surely those at the restaurant realized something was wrong. If not her work colleagues, then Mrs. Jones at the boarding house. Surely noticed? Did they find the keys she dropped on purpose?

All these questions swirled around in her head. Vera tried to calm her mind, but it wasn't working. Hopefully keeping busy in the kitchen would be the relief she needed.

"Here we are," Tyler said cheerfully, as though he was glad to be rid of her. Happy to have the burden of Vera Bailey off his hands.

As they stepped into the kitchen, Joey greeted them. He had a huge grin on his face. "Welcome, welcome," he said cheerfully. He seemed genuinely happy to see her. "Do you mind doing the menial tasks?" He winced as he said the words. It was as though he was apologizing for taking away her boredom.

Vera sighed heavily. She felt relief, just being in here. The aroma alone drew her in. But the man at the helm of this important room also interested her.

He always seemed to be cheerful and happy. Whether that was just for show, for Vera alone, she wasn't sure. She would probably never know.

"I will do whatever you ask," Vera said. Joey handed her an apron. Tying it quickly around her waist, Vera waited for instructions.

"We have a busy night ahead," Joey told her, then pulled some pages toward himself. "This evening, we have the high rollers. They get the best of the best." He glanced across to Tyler.

Tyler nodded. "That is still the case," he said. "At least it's not too big a group. Otherwise, it could be chaotic."

"My kitchen is *never* chaotic. Now that I have an assistant chef," he glanced across to Vera knowingly, "things will be even better."

Vera's heart pounded. She stared at him. What did Tyler tell the chef? She was far from an assistant chef but could certainly help with simple things. "Not... Not a chef, or an assistant chef" she whispered. Now she was scared. Terrified of the expectations put upon her.

Joey put a hand to her shoulder. "I didn't mean to scare you," he said. "I was trying to make a joke, but it didn't come out that way."

Vera was relieved. "Thank goodness," she said. "For a minute there I was worried. I can do basic cooking, I can peel vegetables and do a few other things around the kitchen like washing dishes," she said.

Tyler glanced from one to the other of them. A small smile graced his lips, but it was gone as quickly as it arrived. "If you don't need me, I have things to do. Organization for tonight," he said as way of explanation. Moments later he was gone. He'd left the kitchen, and left Vera alone with Joey.

Joey glanced down at her. Then pushed the pages toward her. "This is what we are creating for tonight. The guests Tyler has coming this evening, are big spenders. Hence the menu."

Vera looked again at the menu in front of her. She'd only glanced before, but now she studied it. Even the restaurant she worked in did not supply such fancy foods to their customers. The first item on the list was soup. Chicken and vegetable soup—it sounded delicious.

Roast beef with potatoes, carrots and beans, all topped with a rich gravy. Followed by dessert of cherry cobbler and clotted cream. Nothing but the best.

Last on the list was cheese and crackers. Who in their right mind, would be able to fit in cheese and crackers after all that food? She glanced up at Joey. She'd felt him watching her the whole time she read through the menu. Now he seemed to be waiting for her response. "It sounds delicious," she said. "It's a lot of food though. Will Tyler's guests be able to eat all that?

Joey grinned. "There are rarely leftovers. The roast is in the oven, has been for hours. That's one thing off our list already. We'll start at the beginning and prepare the chicken for the soup." Joey walked across the kitchen and came back with a cooked chicken that was still warm. "We need to tear the meat from the carcass. Then roughly chop it. On the stove," he said, looking over his shoulder, "are split peas. By now, they will be soft. The chicken stock is already in the pot. Throw the diced chicken in with it. You'll also add carrots, onions, and celery, and a few pinches of salt. Then leave it to boil."

Vera took a moment to take it all in. She went over it in her mind—chicken, carrots, onions, celery, salt. She could do that.

"I'll grab those vegetables, and you can start on that now if you wouldn't mind." Joey looked at her expectantly. It was as though he trusted her to do exactly what he asked.

His trust went a long way. Vera felt a confidence she hadn't felt for a long time. She began to pull the chicken apart, she put it on a board and diced it roughly. She followed Joey's instructions as best she could. Vera had no intention of letting him down.

Joey was being kind to her. He let her into his kitchen, which from what she saw he didn't do often. If she did a good job today, perhaps he would allow her to come back.

There was nothing Vera would not do for Joey. Tyler, too. The two men had gone out of their way to help her, to ensure her safety, and Vera would do whatever she could to pay them back.

With the chicken now ready, she carried it over to the pot and added it. Then she stirred the mix. Vera leaned over the boiling pot, breathed in the aroma. Already it smelled good, and there was still a lot to add. She gave it another stir, then returned to her work bench.

Carrots were next, since they took the longest to cook, and then the onions. What she was doing now, was better than boredom anytime. Hopefully her stint down here in the kitchen meant she would not have so much time on her hands to stare out the window.

Looking for Horace Dalton.

Chapter Fourteen

Tyler was restless, and he didn't know why. He paced the floor of his office, except it was too small to really do much for him.

He sat down and shuffled papers around the desk. He stood, but that didn't help either. Not sure what the cause of his anxiety was, he strolled out of his office. The kitchen wasn't far away.

As he got closer, Tyler heard laughter, along with the rattle of pots and pans. He was on the verge of strolling in uninvited but thought the better of it. It was nice to hear Vera laugh, assuming it was her. Joey was a good man, and he was clearly keeping her entertained.

They had several guests coming tonight, returning guests. They expected the best of everything, since they were paying a high price to be here. He glanced across at the kitchen again, and began to walk there, but stopped when the laughter started again.

He was almost at the door, and even from here, the enticing aroma drifted out into the foyer. Tyler dearly wanted to go in there. To see Vera smiling, to see her happy. It was the one thing he could say he'd never seen on her.

Taking two more steps forward, Tyler pushed himself hard against the wall. He didn't want anyone to witness his anxiety. He now realized he had to admit, if only to himself, he was more interested in Vera then he let on.

There was something about her, he couldn't put his finger on it, but it would come to him. Should he go in and check everything was alright? Except Tyler knew that was the worst thing he could do. He had entrusted her to Joey, and he had to let that play out in whatever way it happened.

"Oh, Tyler! There you are, I was about to come to your office." Harry Johnson, the guard who was previously looking out for Vera was now looking for him. Within moments, Tyler was certain he'd been found out by the pair in the kitchen. When this man spoke, he bellowed. Not that he meant to, that was just his normal voice.

Suddenly you could hear a pin drop, and the door to the kitchen opened. Joey stepped out, curiosity written all over his face. Tyler didn't say a word, he waited for Joey to berate him for watching them. Only Joey did no such thing.

"Your girl is doing well," Joey told him. "Come in and see for yourself."

Even before Joey finished the sentence, Tyler was shaking his head. He didn't want Vera to think he was spying on her, checking that she was doing alright. He began walking away in the opposite direction to the kitchen. "I'm pleased it's worked out," Tyler said. "Not only for your benefit, but also for Vera. She needed a break from the tedium."

Joey ran a hand through his hair and gazed at Tyler. "This is not about me Tyler. It's all about looking after Vera. She's having a great time in there, and I don't want anything to spoil it for her."

Tyler wasn't sure what to say to that. If he didn't know better, he'd think Joey was pining after Vera. Joey had never been particularly good with people, and hiding away in the kitchen was one way he dealt with it.

"I want her to be happy, not terrified all the time," Tyler said to his friend. "It sounds like she would be delighted to come back again tomorrow?" He couldn't give any reason why either one of them would refuse. Especially since they seem to get on so well together.

Joey opened his mouth to speak then closed it again. It made Tyler wonder what it was he was going to divulge. He must have changed his mind because then he spoke again. "Vera has made the most wonderful chicken soup for tonight. You should come and check it out, your guests will love it."

"Perhaps later when I'm not so busy," Tyler told him. "I have to work on the security for tonight. I'll try to catch up in a while." Joey nodded, and Tyler strode in the opposite direction.

If he didn't know better Tyler would believe he was jealous of Joey. Of the time he and Vera were spending together. Except that couldn't be true, he had no feelings for Vera. He glanced back over his shoulder and saw Joey watching him. He quickly turned away.

He had important work to do, and it was time he went and did it.

As much as he didn't want to leave, Tyler headed to his office. His head of security, Harry Johnson, was waiting there for him. The two men leaned over the rough drawing Harry had brought with him. Tyler studied it for long moments, then glanced up at Harry.

Tyler's gaze went back to the large paper sitting on his desk. In his mind, he was testing out each position his security guards would be in. He always had plenty of security, simply because some gamblers were volatile. "What about this spot?" Tyler's finger pointed to an entry that was not covered. "Normally I'd say it was enough, but with Vera here..." He didn't finish the sentence. He didn't need to.

Harry totally understood since he was the one who had been guarding Vera all this time. "I can put more men on if you want me to," he said. "It will cost more that's all." He studied Tyler then, waiting for a response.

Of course, Tyler was willing to pay the extra. Money meant little to him. "Whatever you need. My only concern is keeping Vera safe. Your men need to be on the lookout for Horace Dalton." Harry nodded. He'd worked for Tyler long enough now to know how passionate his boss was about such things.

Tyler lifted a pencil and handed it to his head of security. "I'd like to see extra security here, here, and here," he said pointing to each of those places.

Harry tilted his head slightly. "If that's what you want, that's what you'll get. It just seems a lot of extra..."

"Don't argue," Tyler said sternly. "A woman's life is in danger, and we need to ensure Horace cannot get into this building. If he has even an inkling of her being here, he'll find a way to get inside." Harry stared at him; it was clear he did not understand how determined Horace Dalton could be. Tyler stood straight and stretched his shoulders. He glared at the other man. Harry moved back a step or two. Something he'd never done before, but then again,

Tyler was not normally so assertive. The situation called for extreme action.

"Whatever you say, Boss." Harry put his hands up in front of him, signaling his defeat.

Tyler studied him for a moment or two but knew Harry would follow his instructions. He tilted his head, indicating clear understanding.

Harry rolled up his roughly drawn map of the building, and quietly left the office. Tyler breathed a sigh of relief—as much as he knew Harry didn't agree with him, he was acutely aware the other man would follow his orders.

Even if those orders seemed overly excessive or unnecessary.

Tyler sat down at his desk. He was lost and wasn't sure what to do next. Never in his life had he felt this way. It could be because of the danger his staff were in.

Or was it because of the stranger currently cooking in his kitchen? Tyler decided he may never know.

Chapter Fifteen

Vera heard someone speak Tyler's name and stopped what she was doing. Moments ago, she was laughing, having fun with Joey. She knew she shouldn't as she was in so much danger, but she couldn't help it. Once you got to know him, Joey was a great person. He was also an excellent chef. She knew that firsthand.

She finished preparing all the vegetables for the soup, and only needed to stir it every now and then. The aroma from that chicken soup was extremely enticing. It was also easy to make, she would have to keep that recipe in her mind for future use.

Joey stepped outside the kitchen, to see what all the commotion was about. He sent Vera into the pantry to hide, just in case. Neither of them was prepared to say what they thought. That perhaps Horace Dalton had found his way inside.

She hurried into the pantry, the same room she'd hidden in with Tyler when he'd first saved her. Her heart was pounding, and her head was spinning. She was more worried for Tyler and Joey than she was for herself. If Horace Dalton had found his way in here, he would eliminate the two men before he did anything else.

Those two men, who were near enough to strangers, were willing to protect her with their lives. Except Vera could not allow that. If it came down to that, she would give herself up.

She heard Joey's voice. It was a low whisper, and she couldn't make out the words.

The conversation lasted only a short time. Joey returned to the kitchen far quicker than she'd expected. Vera stepped out of the pantry, expecting to be admonished by Joey. He was like a big brother to her—protective and loving all at once. He'd even hugged her when she'd felt low.

She enjoyed being here in the kitchen, not only because it gave her something to do, but because of the company. "Is everything all right?" She couldn't help but ask. Vera was so fearful for everyone else. She still worried about herself, of course, but to put others in danger... That truly upset her.

Joey studied her and seemed to think carefully about his words. "Just Tyler being Tyler. He's often like this before a big night. Tonight's guests are big spenders, hence the extra special menu. We go all out for them. They get the best food, and the best wine. They are also placed in the best room."

Vera was completely confused. "What exactly is it Tyler does here?" she asked. Almost immediately Vera wished she could take the words back. It really wasn't her business.

Joey tilted his head to the side and studied her. "You really don't know? Tyler is a gambler. This place" he spread his hands indicating the building, "it's all about gambling. Men come from miles away to gamble. Tonight's guests are what we call high rollers. They are the big spenders and have money to burn."

"And the accommodations upstairs?" Vera was more confused than ever. But then it suddenly hit her. She'd been in one of those gambling rooms, except she didn't know what it was at the time. "I think Tyler took me to one of those rooms when I first arrived.," she said. "Then he changed his mind and took me to one of the bedrooms. The honeymoon suite he called it."

Joey grinned. "It is the honeymoon suite you are staying in. It's the best room in the place. Most gamblers don't stay here, and then it's only if they are invited."

Vera grimaced. "Does that mean I've caused someone to be put out of their bed?" It was the last thing she wanted. And she certainly didn't want Tyler losing money because of her. "You have both gone to so much trouble because of me. I feel so bad." Tears filled her eyes. "I... I should just leave. There must be a way to get away from here without Horace Dalton finding me."

She really didn't want to leave, both men had made her feel comfortable here. Wanted. And Joey made her feel needed. He didn't need her help in the kitchen. He'd managed alone all this time, but having her here? That was a bonus he told her. She was enjoying it, So, what was the harm?

Joey frowned. He opened his arms wide. Not saying a word, he pulled her into him and wrapped his arms around her. "It is not safe to leave," he said firmly. "We will look after you here. Tyler has a team of security guards. Between us all you are safe."

Vera glanced up at him. "Security guards?"

Joey patted her back. "Of course. Gambling is volatile, sometimes people get violent. Tyler needs to ensure the safety of all players, not to mention himself and his staff."

Her heart pounded, Vera didn't know what to say. So instead, she said nothing, and rested her head against Joey's chest. The feeling of him being a big brother kicked in again. Strangely, she did not feel that way about Tyler.

What she felt for him, should not be vocalized. Vera knew if she told herself that enough times, it may become fact. She was only here for a short time, a few days at most. Above all, she knew there was no way Tyler was interested in her as a woman. He only saw her as a damsel in distress.

It was something she'd never been, and never wanted to be. Except here she was, relying on him to keep her safe. To keep her away from the man who'd harmed her. Joey's grasp on her loosened. She didn't want to move away from him, she felt comfortable right where she was.

When this was all over, she would leave and go back to Eden. Back to her job and to her room at the boarding house, where all her friends were.

She glanced up at him, and he looked down into her face. "This has been nice," he said with a grin on his face. "But we have work to do, and we need to get back to it if we are to have the meal ready on time."

Of course, Joey was right, besides, they couldn't stand around all day like this. Someone might get the wrong idea. Someone like Tyler, for instance. She wouldn't know how to explain it to him.

Vera nodded. She could do little else, as she knew Joey was right. They had a lot of work ahead of them. It wasn't that she minded the work, it was just that she was comfortable in his arms.

The kitchen door suddenly opened. It was thrown back with force, and the pair were startled. Joey snatched up a large kitchen knife and pushed her to the floor. Vera's heart pounded. Now she worried about Joey's safety, despite the oversized kitchen knife in his hand.

What he intended to do with it she wasn't sure. She couldn't see what was going on, but Joey had one hand on her shoulder keeping her down and out of sight. Vera felt ill, she swallowed back the bile that threatened to surface.

She glanced up at Joey, his concentration was on the person who entered the kitchen. Except Vera couldn't see who that was. Not from here. And Joey had pressure on her shoulder, which meant she couldn't stand.

She was grateful to him, there was no doubt about that. Except she had no intention of letting him die for her. She had to find a way to get out of his grip and show herself.

Vera somehow wriggled from beneath Joey's hold on her and managed to stand up. That's when she saw him.

Chapter Sixteen

Tyler rushed into the kitchen. "What do you think you're doing?" he demanded. This man was one of his security guards. He was new, but he had clearly not listened to the instructions given to him by Harry.

"My apologies," the man said. "I'm…Apparently, I'm lost."

Anger rushed through Tyler. Vera didn't need this, neither did Joey. His eyes turned towards the pair. It was then he noticed the large knife in Joey's hand.

Vera was white as a ghost, and she had both hands in the air. Did that mean she was surrendering? At that moment he realized she'd thought this was Horace Dalton come to get her. Did she not know Tyler would not allow that to happen?

He turned to the guard again. "Go directly to my office and wait for me there." Even his voice gave away his anger. But this should never have happened. Harry would not have allowed it to happen, which made him wonder if this new man was working for Horace.

Now he felt panicked. What if it was true? What if this man really did work for Horace? As far as Tyler was aware, the new man had only been employed at most a week ago. It may even have been yesterday for all he knew.

He stood frozen to the spot, for all of twenty seconds. Then he stared at Joey. "It's alright, at least I think it is." He then turned and ran from the kitchen, heading back toward his office. Whether the man would be there when he arrived was another thing altogether.

He saw Harry along the way. "You need to come with me," he said. "There's been an incident with one of your men." Tyler didn't wait for Harry to keep up with him, time was of the essence.

"Which one?" Harry called from behind.

"The new one, I don't know his name," Tyler said. "I told him to go to my office. Whether he did is another thing altogether."

Tyler couldn't help himself, he ran as though his life depended on it. Except it was Vera's life that was at stake. When he reached his office, Tyler was surprised to find the man there. He came to a sudden halt, and Harry ran into his back. Tyler breathed a sigh of relief. He was convinced the new man wouldn't be there when he arrived at his office.

He walked in and sat down behind the desk. Harry entered moments later. He stared at the new man, now unsure. Tyler was surprised, because Harry was always so careful checking on new people. He usually only took people who'd been recommended. And those recommendations had to come from people Tyler knew. That way they were somewhat accountable for the recommendations they provided.

Tyler stared at the new man. "What is your name," he asked, this time he was a bit more amenable. He had calmed down a little since walking into his office and seeing the man there.

"Tony," the man said. "Tony Jansen. I'm really sorry, I didn't mean to barge in like that. I guess I got lost," he said, sounding very genuine. Tyler truly hoped he was.

He glanced at Harry. This was his department, and he needed to sort it out. "I'll leave it to you Harry," Tyler said. "I have a lot to do to prepare for tonight. Just make sure he knows what he's doing before tonight, otherwise he has to go." He stormed out of the room leaving Harry to sort out his new security guard.

Tyler went straight to the front door. He had to ensure it was locked. He also needed reassurance this man had not been employed by Horace Dalton, to abduct Vera again. He had left strict instructions the door was to be kept locked at all times. It normally was when there was no game going on, but still, it was better safe than sorry.

Once he checked the door and was happy it was secure, he returned to the kitchen. His heart was still pounding, he'd had a terrible fright. He was certain Vera would be feeling the same. Joey too.

He opened the door to the kitchen, only he was far more gentle than it had been opened earlier. He felt frazzled and very stressed. Which wasn't surprising. He walked over to the large kitchen counter.

Joey looked up from what he was doing. "Tea, coffee?"

Vera was sipping on a mug of tea. Tyler didn't blame her. She must have got a terrible fright having someone storm into the kitchen like that. "I really need something stronger," Tyler said. "But coffee better do." Joey turned away to pour his coffee. Tyler reached out and took a mouthful the moment it hit the counter.

Before he had a chance to speak again, Joey beat him to it. "We are both fine. We did get a fright, but we have recovered suitably. Any idea what happened?"

Tyler took another sip of coffee before answering. He rolled his eyes. "According to Harry, he's new.

The guard has apologized, and I've left him with Harry. He will sort him out one way or the other." He glanced at Vera. She looked upset.

"You're not going to sack him, are you? It will be another thing on my conscience if you do."

Tyler was confused. Why she thought he would sack the man, he didn't know. Except he did. He was furious when he was there the last time, when the new guard had breached the kitchen. It was an unfortunate incident, but hopefully by now, Harry had it all sorted. He would not put up with this sort of nonsense, just as Tyler wouldn't.

"I've left it to Harry to decide what he's doing," Tyler said. "It's his department.

Vera nodded, but did not look appeased. She stared down into the mug of tea. Why she thought it was her fault, Tyler didn't know. Except maybe she thought none of this would have happened if it weren't for her presence here. She would be wrong.

Now he had to prove he was worthy of the job of her protector.

It wasn't that hard a job to do, not normally. Except he had to admit, the building was large, there were a lot of hallways, and a lot of rooms going off those hallways. If you're new, it was probably a lot to take in. In hindsight he could have said so, but at the time all he could see was white fury.

He glanced across at Joey, who had said little except to offer him coffee. As he glanced across at Joey, his eyes were saying be gentle. "Harry won't sack him, he never does. He wouldn't have employed the man if he didn't think he could do the job."

Every word Joey said was true. Harry was selective. If there was even the slightest doubt in his mind, he would not have given Tony Janson the job.

He heard Vera sigh. He hoped Joey's words helped. "Are you enjoying your time in here?" He wasn't sure what else to say, given the circumstances. So perhaps his question would be twofold. Firstly, to help calm her, as it did him. Secondly, to let Tyler know whether he should send her here again tomorrow.

A smile crossed her face. "I love it down here," she said. "Can I come back tomorrow?" Her gaze went from Tyler to Joey. Her smile faded. It was built of concern he was certain.

"Definitely," Joey said before Tyler had a chance to answer. "You are the best assistant chef I have ever had in this kitchen." He was grinning now.

Not that Tyler would say, but Vera was the only assistant chef Joey had ever had in his kitchen. He had never allowed Tyler to give him an assistant. It was far too much trouble he'd always said. And now, here he was enjoying every moment of it.

"Finish your coffee and get going," Joey said, half joking. "We still have a lot of work to do before tonight's dinner."

Tyler grinned. His heart rate had slowed. Just spending time with these two had helped, but he knew more than anything, Vera was the one who really helped. Just being in the room with her was... special.

Chapter Seventeen

Vera drank down the last of her tea. It had taken some time, but her heart rate had finally reduced. She wondered about Joey. He must have been terrified, holding that large knife, not to mention pushing her down to the floor and ensuring she stayed there. As much as she was grateful to him, she was also annoyed as he'd taken her choices away.

After Tyler had left the kitchen, she turned to Joey. "What would you like me to do next," she asked.

Joey thought for a moment. "We have a lot of vegetables to peel, perhaps start with those. After that we'll work on the cherry cobbler."

Vera was happy to do anything that was needed. Working beside Joey had alleviated her boredom. He directed her to a large wooden box in the corner, where she found a mixture of vegetables including potatoes and carrots. She placed them in a basket and carried them across to the work counter.

"Tonight will be busy," Joey told her. "I know you are an experienced waitress, but you will not be waitressing tonight. You also won't be alone in this kitchen."

Vera knew what Joey was getting at. She was going to be locked in the room again. She sighed. She totally understood the reasoning, but with all the guards Tyler had, why was this necessary? This was not something Joey had decided, she was certain.

Tyler was the one who made these kinds of decisions, and mostly they'd been good. But this one, this one was awful. "It doesn't make sense," she said gruffly. She stared up at Joey. His eyes were sad. That told her he didn't agree either. Or maybe he did and didn't want to say.

Joey shrugged his shoulders. "It's for your safety," he said firmly. "Neither of us want to see you harmed. The decision has been made and it won't be reversed."

Vera had never seen him so adamant. She had only been here a few short days, but she'd become close with Joey. He was the big brother she'd never had but had always wanted.

Tyler, on the other hand, was the opposite. Tingles ran down her spine whenever he was near. She knew exactly what that meant, but did not want to admit it to herself, let alone to Tyler.

Besides, she would be gone as soon as Horace Dalton was caught. How long that would be, was the question. In some ways she wished he would try to get in tonight. Perhaps he would try to come in with the crowd, if that's even the way this worked. She really had no idea.

"How many of these do you want peeled?" Now she changed the subject. She didn't like putting Joey in such a position. One where he got annoyed with her. Not that he was really annoyed, it was more like he became defensive. She hadn't seen him like that before.

"All of them," Joey said, not even looking at her. Had she ruined their relationship with her impetuous behavior? She hoped not. Joey held a special place in her heart.

They continued preparing the meal in silence. Vera was heartbroken. She was now certain she had caused too much damage to their relationship, and they would never be the same again.

Vera felt uneasy. She didn't want it to be like this. She placed the small knife and the potato she was peeling, on the counter. "How many players will there be tonight?" she asked.

Joey glanced at her, but didn't stop what he was doing. "There will be ten, provided they all turn up. There is a large fee to join, so they inevitably all come." He immediately went back to what he was doing, which was preparing the cherry cobbler.

Now she understood how Tyler made his money. Vera had believed it was from gambling, but it seems the fee was really how he did it. She wondered if he joined in the game, but didn't ask.

"Look," Joey said, this time facing her. "I'm sorry about before. We really are trying our best to protect you, and your skills would be gratefully appreciated, but…" He wiped his hands on his apron. "Who knows what these gamblers will share with outsiders? Your situation is precarious already. Let's not make it worse."

Vera knew Joey was right. Putting herself in such a position could be the end of her. Not to mention putting others in danger, too. Horace Dalton couldn't be trusted. He was the worst type of criminal there was. He didn't care who he harmed to get his way.

She gazed into Joey's face. "I understand," she whispered.

He opened his arms, and she stepped into the comfort he offered. All was right with her world again. At least her relationship with Joey had been restored. At this moment in time, that's all that mattered.

~*~

It had been a long day, but to Vera it was worth it. All the food was ready, except for the cheese and crackers. They would do those at the last minute, so the cheese didn't dry out. There was still plenty of time before the gamblers arrived, and she was thrilled to discover she was to help Joey set the tables.

This was her area of expertise. Joey led her up to the room they would be using tonight. One of the guards tagged along with them, just to be certain they were safe. Not that she expected anything to happen. Not now anyway. Perhaps later Horace Dalton might try to trick his way in.

The mere thought of it had her heart racing.

"Everything we need for the tables is in this cupboard," Joey told her, indicating the cupboard in question.

Vera opened the door, and almost squealed. Everything was high class. She had never seen such beautiful tablecloths and napkins. Even the glassware and cutlery were the best of the best.

This room was separate to the gambling room. She hadn't noticed it when she'd been brought here when she first arrived, but there was a door beside the bar that led into here. It made sense. They couldn't clear the tables of cards to eat.

"They will eat before they play," Joey said. "That's the way they do it, I guess so they don't interrupt the games."

It made sense to Vera. She had wondered how they organized the night. This was a whole new situation for her. Although she had been waitressing for many years, and doing it successfully, it was at a restaurant. This was a completely different scenario.

The table was large, every bit as big as the one in the gambling room. She pulled out a tablecloth, and with the flick of a wrist, spread it over the table. She snatched up the cutlery and placed it perfectly on the table. Next was napkins, and then the glassware.

She glanced up to see Joey staring at her, his mouth gaping.

"Well, that's a new one," he said. "I've never seen a table set so quickly."

Vera smiled. "It comes with experience. Is it appropriate to have a centerpiece?" She didn't want to breach protocol. She figured in this situation, a centerpiece was not normally used.

"No centerpiece." Joey was firm about that, and Vera could understand why.

"I guess it's not something men like," she said.

Joey grinned. "These men like to think they are very masculine." He laughed then, and warmth filled Vera.

The coldness she had felt in the kitchen earlier had now lifted. She was glad they'd cleared the air. She enjoyed being with Joey, and didn't want that to end.

Chapter Eighteen

Tyler was sitting quietly in his office, checking last minute details, when there was a knock at the door. He glanced up. Harry Johnson was there, along with one of his security guards. This particular guard had been with him for a long time. Almost since the beginning of Tyler's business opening.

He waved his hand for them to enter and stopped what he was doing.

The two men entered but hovered in the doorway. "What can I do for you?" Tyler asked, impatient to get back to what he was doing.

Harry appeared nervous and ran a hand through his hair. "It's about Horace," he said firmly. "This young fella is a relative."

Tyler stared at him. He knew this guard and knew him well. It was highly unlikely he would betray Tyler. He'd always been honest and hardworking. "Jason, isn't it?" He indicated for both men to sit down.

"Yes, Sir. Jason Gawne," the other man said. "Horace is a distant cousin. Very distant. No one in the family will have anything to do with him." He straightened his shoulders and gazed directly at Tyler. "There's been a whisper, I thought you should know."

Tyler waited impatiently. He wasn't sure why Jason stopped talking. Perhaps he was worried about his job? "Your job is safe," Tyler told him. "Go ahead and tell me what you know."

Jason sighed, then stared Tyler in the eyes. "I heard he's going to try and get in tonight, when the gamblers arrive."

"There will be several men on the door, so it should be safe." This information was nothing new, so Tyler was unsure why these two were here.

Jason squirmed in the chair, clearly uncomfortable. "The word is he's going to kidnap one of the gamblers and take his place. Nothing would surprise me, the man is bad. I'm ashamed to even say we're related."

Tyler was speechless. They would have to be extra careful, but without knowing which gambler Horace was going to target, he didn't know how to keep the man safe. "Thank you, Jason," Tyler said. "I will remember this. Your loyalty will not go unrewarded."

Jason stood abruptly and glanced down at Tyler. "I didn't do it for reward," he said. "I did it to protect that lady, Vera, and to hopefully see Horace behind bars. Finally."

Tyler couldn't help but be impressed with this young man. He would find a way to reward him despite what Jason said.

Harry followed Jason's lead and stood. Tyler wasn't certain he wanted them to leave, particularly Jason. Presumably, he knew Horace well, even if he had little to do with him. "I'd like Jason to stay, if that's alright," Tyler told Harry.

"Of course," Harry said. "Who am I to argue?"

Jason sat down again, although he didn't seem comfortable with this change of events. "Don't worry, I just want to ask you a few things," Tyler told him. "My first question is, how long since you have seen Horace? Would you recognize him if you saw him now?"

Jason thought for a moment or two. He rubbed a hand across his chin. "It's probably been a couple of years at least," Jason told him. "But yes, I'm sure I would recognize him. You want me to point him out?" he asked, his voice incredulous.

Tyler wasn't sure what he wanted Jason to do. He felt there was little they could do, until the time came for his guests to arrive. "You know the situation, what I need is someone I can trust. Vera, the lady in question, needs protection. I think you are the one to do it."

Jason's face was blank, and Tyler wasn't sure what that meant. "You want me... To protect this lady, despite Horace being my cousin."

"Distant cousin?" Tyler asked. He wouldn't contemplate it if they had been close, but from what Jason had told him, that wasn't the case.

Jason nodded. "You can trust me to look after her, I promise you that."

Tyler studied him, he wasn't one to trust easily. Particularly when someone's life was at stake, as it was now. "I will take you to the kitchen and introduce you to Vera. She will be going back to her room before our guests arrive."

He stared at Jason as he seemed to be deciding something. Then he opened his mouth to speak. "As I said earlier, I haven't seen Horace for at least two years, but I wouldn't put it past him to come early. To catch us off guard."

Tyler wouldn't either. Horace was as sneaky as they came. Nothing he did would surprise Tyler, and apparently the same went for Jason. "You could be right," he told the guard. "What we do about it, is the question. Let's go to the kitchen now, then we'll think about that dilemma."

Tyler stood and Jason followed, then they both left the office. They headed for the kitchen, Tyler's mind in a whirl. He had it all worked out, how tonight was going to go. This put a spanner in the works, but it was better than being caught off guard.

The moment they entered the kitchen, Vera's head shot up. Joey's too. Tyler led Jason to the counter where they worked and introduced them. "Jason will be guarding you tonight," Tyler said. Vera looked none too happy, but it was what it was. He noticed her hands shaking.

"Coffee?" Joey asked.

Jason looked confused. He obviously didn't want to upset Tyler. "Always," Tyler said. "It's been a particularly difficult day, so coffee would definitely be appreciated."

Joey turned away and filled two mugs with coffee and returned to the counter. He turned away again, this time returning with pastries. "Help yourselves," he said, pushing the plate toward the pair.

"This is one of those rewards I was talking about earlier," Tyler told Jason. "Only I was thinking of something a little more pricey. I'm not sure what yet."

"I told you I don't need a reward," Jason said, looking particularly uncomfortable.

"I will work it out, you'll see." Tyler was adamant Jason would be appropriately rewarded for the information he provided. He turned to Joey and Vera. "Jason has provided crucial information about Horace, and what he plans to do tonight."

Vera looked terrified.

"I promise to take good care of you, Miss Vera," Jason said.

Tyler wasn't certain his promise would help, but it was a step in the right direction.

Chapter Nineteen

Vera couldn't stop shaking, and her mind was in a whirl. What crucial information? What did this Jason know that Tyler wasn't telling her?

She couldn't believe her ears. She wanted to object, to demand she be told what was going on. Except her body was not cooperating. Vera felt an arm wind around her shoulders. She was pulled close and held tight. She glanced up to see Joey looking down at her. "Everything will be alright," he said. "You will be safe. Totally protected. Isn't that right, Tyler?"

Her eyes turned to Tyler who appeared frustrated. On second thought, he seemed annoyed. Was that because Joey was holding her? Tyler had never attempted to console Vera, even when she needed it the most.

She had no interest in Joey except as a friend. Tyler on the other hand sent chills down her spine when he was near. However, it didn't appear any such thing happened to him when Vera was around.

Joey's hands rubbed circles over her back. "Feeling any better?" he whispered, so only Vera could hear.

She nodded. "I'm fine," Vera told him quietly, although she really wasn't.

As though he saw right through her, Joey poured her a fresh mug of tea. "Thank you," she whispered, then took a sip. It was strange how tea could make everything better.

Joey stared at Tyler. "We really need to finish up here. That is if you want the meals to be ready on time."

Tyler frowned. Joey looked indifferent.

It told Vera he knew exactly what he was doing. His plan was clearly to get Tyler and Jason out of the kitchen. That way she would not be so upset. It wasn't the food Joey was worried about. It was Vera.

They were almost done with the preparation for the evening meals. But Tyler didn't know that. He was distracted. Vera knew, from what he'd said earlier, he had a lot of organization to do for the night's proceedings.

The worst part was knowing Horace still had his eyes on her. Figuratively, that was. While ever she was available, he would try to retrieve her. He'd snatched her once, what was stopping him from doing the same thing again?

The half-full mug of tea was slammed onto the kitchen top. The liquid slopped over the sides, but it didn't deter Vera. She didn't so much as glance at Joey. Instead, she ran out of the kitchen and caught up with Tyler and Jason.

She was breathless, and her words came out disjointed. "If I was married, would Horace continue to chase me?"

She was addressing Jason, but Tyler stared at her, his mouth gaping. "But you're not. Married that is."

Jason studied her for a moment or two. He shook his head. "He never touches married women. At least that's what I was told. He worries about their husbands coming after him. Besides," he said, then paused momentarily.

It made Vera wonder what he was going to say.

"Besides, he prefers his women to be pure when they come to him." His face turned beet red, and it was clear just saying those words to her was embarrassing.

Tyler turned to Jason. "Thank you for your honesty. Please wait for me in my office." He waited long enough for Jason to be out of earshot before speaking. "If it takes you being married, I can arrange for it to happen," Tyler said matter-of-factly.

It wasn't something Vera wanted to do but if it meant keeping her safe, then wasn't it worth the effort? Except it seemed he wasn't so keen. It made

Vera wonder how Joey would react if she asked him to marry her. She would, of course, suggest a marriage of convenience until she was certain she was safe.

Tyler, who was always so certain about everything, came across differently this time. It was blatantly obvious he didn't want to marry her, even for a marriage of convenience they could easily annul.

She didn't say a word but turned and stormed away. Vera went into the kitchen and sidled up to Joey. "I need to get married," she said, still slightly breathless. "I don't think Tyler is interested."

Joey raised his eyebrows. "That's a surprise," he said. "He's clearly in love with you."

That was news to Vera, and she told Joey so. "Haven't you seen the way he looks at you? Or the longing in his eyes?" He chuckled, and as he did, the kitchen door flew open.

"I'll do it," Tyler said forcefully. "I've arranged for the preacher to come here shortly."

Joey chuckled again. "You're too late. She's asked me," he told Tyler, despite it not being true.

Vera watched as Tyler grimaced. She wasn't sure what it meant. Was he annoyed Joey had beaten him to it, or was he relieved. Either way, she wasn't sure what would happen now. Instead of getting in the middle of a discussion about who would marry her, if anyone, she went to the stove and stirred the soup. After all the work she put into it, Vera had no intention of letting it burn.

Both men lowered their voices. They were quiet enough Vera couldn't hear what they were saying. Every now and then, one of them became a little louder. Were they arguing? It sounded to be more than a friendly discussion.

She stayed at the stove to avoid both men while they were discussing which of them would marry her. If either one did.

Perhaps it wasn't such a good idea after all?

Vera reached for a spoon and lifted some of the soup to her mouth. The aroma was amazing. The fact it had been cooking much of the day had helped. She blew on the spoon to cool it down. She was anxious to try it.

She turned to face the two men as she did so. They were still in a deep conversation. Whether that was about her or something entirely different, Vera didn't know. She lifted the soup to her mouth again and took a sip.

Delicious.

It was a pity she wouldn't get to eat it. The guests would have a wholesome meal though. And that's what really mattered.

Chapter Twenty

Tyler was becoming annoyed. At no time had he told Vera he wouldn't marry her. Only he didn't want it to be temporary. He was certain that's what she was suggesting.

Even in the short time he'd had her hidden away here, he'd fallen in love with her. It was evident to Tyler, she was in love with Joey, and that complicated things.

Except Joey denied the allegations. He insisted he was more of a brother figure to Vera. Tyler wasn't convinced.

"If that were the case," Joey said, trying to keep his voice low, "why did she come running out to you with the suggestion? Why didn't she stay here in the kitchen and ask me?"

Tyler couldn't argue with that, but he did. "Who knows what goes through her head?" he asked. "It's a confusing time."

"You are the most foolish man I've ever had the misfortune to meet!" Joey threw down the kitchen towel he held and stormed away. Tyler watched as Joey went to the stove where Vera was tasting the soup.

"It's delicious," he heard her say. "Try some."

Joey reached for a clean spoon, his eyes on Tyler the entire time. He took a sip. "It's good. You did well. I would happily have you in my kitchen each and every day," he said loudly. Ensuring Tyler could hear.

Tyler strode across the room and joined the pair at the stove. "May I try?" he asked, ensuring he did not look at Joey. He was annoyed with the chef, his closest friend, even if Joey was telling the truth. Or at least what Joey believed to be the truth.

Vera offered a spoonful of the chicken soup to him, and Tyler leaned closer. So close, he was mesmerized by the aroma. Or perhaps he was charmed by the woman holding out the sample to him.

"Wonderful," Tyler said after accepting the mouthful of chicken and vegetable soup. "My guests will adore this."

Vera glanced at Joey, who grinned. "Vera is a wonderful cook," the chef said. "I want her in my kitchen every day from now on."

At first Tyler was annoyed. Did it mean Joey was aiming to move in and win over Vera's affections? Or was Tyler being paranoid?

If he asked, Tyler knew his friend would tell him in no uncertain terms he was obsessed. "The preacher is arranged," Tyler said out of the blue. "He should be here soon. I'm sorry you will be locked in your room for the evening, but it can't be helped." He truly was sorry. No woman should be treated in such a way, especially on her wedding night.

Vera scrutinized Tyler until he felt uncomfortable. "There is something you need to know," she said, then stirred the soup once again.

The preacher came and went. Vera seemed happy enough about the marriage, although they'd not discussed anything specific about their future. He did not want a marriage of convenience, but clearly Vera did. For her, it was only about being safe.

For Tyler it was all about the heart. He couldn't concentrate when she was near. When they touched, shivers went down his spine. It was something Tyler had never encountered before in his more than four decades of life.

He felt uneasy about tonight's proceedings, given the information Vera had now shared. Whether she was correct was another thing altogether. She'd been drugged, and her mind in a fog.

Still, she seemed adamant – he had to take it as gospel. It was not worth the risk to do otherwise.

At her request, Vera stayed in the kitchen with Joey for the rest of the day. He also had protection there for her, despite Joey's protests. He was convinced he could protect his new friend, and rightly so.

Except Tyler was not willing to risk her safety. Sheriff Peter Jones was also in the building, fully aware of this new information. Harry Johnson, Tyler's head of security, had been informed, and was not impressed. He prided himself on his ability to ensure all his staff were reliable and truthful.

Less than an hour later, the guests began to arrive. Jason Gawne was placed at the front door until all the guests were inside, since he could identify Horace Dalton.

Vera helped Joey to plate the food, then place it in the dumbwaiter, ready to be delivered to the dining room they'd set up earlier. The metal covers on each plate would keep the food hot.

Now it was show time. Tyler was more nervous than he'd ever been with a group of big gamblers. Except tonight was far more than a night of gambling. It was all about saving Vera's life.

~*~

Tyler gingerly walked up the stairs to Vera's room. His heart hurt worrying about her. He'd been in a lot of dangerous situations over the years, given his occupation. Life as a gambler was not an easy one. There were cheats everywhere, and most were prepared to kill a man rather than admit the truth.

Still, he'd been lucky.

And yet, right now, Tyler was far more worried about the woman he'd only met recently, than he'd ever been about his own life.

He was certain Horace would make his move tonight. Tyler would be distracted with his high rolling guests, and that would suit Horace perfectly. Jason came across as trustworthy and promised to guard Vera with his life.

Harry Johnson stood outside Vera's room, waiting for Tyler to arrive.

The moment he did, Harry opened the door, and the pair went inside. Both Tyler and Harry turned that room upside down, ensuring no one was in there hiding. When they were done, the two men left the room again, and Harry took up his position once more.

It wouldn't be long, and Jason Gawne would arrive to take over.

Tyler's heart pounded.

He glanced up as he heard movement on the stairs. Jason took his time as he headed toward them. "Your guests are safely installed," Jason said, a smile on his face.

Tyler studied him – Jason looked decidedly nervous. "You're not worried about tonight are you, Jason?" Tyler queried. "We've checked the room, and it's all clear. I just need you to stand guard here now. Vera is tired and is going to rest. It's been a long day for her."

"Yes, Sir," Jason said, still sounding anxious.

"I'm glad you're up to the task at hand. I can send someone up to help if you need it?" Tyler was sure his offer would be rejected, and he was correct.

"We'll be off then," Tyler said, his heart pounding. Despite the best laid plans, he was still concerned for Vera's safety. When Horace set his heart on a particular woman, he followed through until the end. Even if it meant he never secured her. There had been cases where it was believed he'd murdered those untouchable women. He would not allow Vera to be one of them.

With Harry Johnson by his side, Tyler hurried down the stairs and waited at the bottom. He had set everything in place, now he could only hope it all played out. They had no choice but to wait.

He would not put Vera's life at risk. Not now, and not ever. Horace Dalton was the worst of the worst and would stop at nothing. Tyler would not allow his wife's life to be put in danger. Tonight's goal was capturing Horace.

There was far more at play tonight that simply arresting Horace. The information that came to light had proven the situation was far more sinister.

As the pair waited at the bottom of the stairs, he heard the click of the bedroom door unlocking. Harry silently signaled the sheriff, who, in turn, signaled his deputies. They crept up the stairs with as much haste as they could without being heard.

Each man had his gun in hand and was prepared for anything. Harry held Tyler back, despite his boss's protests. He wanted to be there to ensure Horace didn't get away. "They'll get him," Harry whispered, and Tyler had to believe it was true.

"You've got it all wrong!" Jason's voice echoed down the stairs.

Tyler knew they hadn't got it wrong. What Vera had seen while still drugged had cleared the way to finally arrest Horace and his cohort.

There was a scuffle, then running down the stairs. Tyler glanced up and used his leg to trip the repulsive older man as he tried to flee. As Horace lay prone on the ground, Tyler pushed his foot to the evil man's back, keeping him there for the sheriff.

It was all he could do not to smash his fist into Horace's face.

"Well, well. What do we have here?" Sheriff Peter Jones asked as he descended the stairs. "Fancy seeing you here, Horace." The smirk on his face told Tyler he couldn't be happier. They had tried to bring this man to justice for decades and had never been able to catch him in the act.

Sheriff Jones pulled Horace to his feet. Moments later, Jason Gawne was led out in handcuffs too. If Vera had not recalled seeing Jason when Horace kidnapped her, he shuddered to think where she would be now.

Earlier, when he'd entered the kitchen, Vera had visible shivers going through her. At first, she didn't know the reason. It had come to her later, when she'd run out of the kitchen. His aroma was what nailed it. Away from the various smells in the kitchen, she got a real whiff of the man, and it all came flooding back.

Working for Tyler had been a good cover. No one suspected he was working for Horace. Especially when he pretended to hate the man. He was a little too forceful about his hatred for his supposedly distance cousin. On checking, the sheriff discovered there was no family relationship between the two men.

Only a business one.

Chapter Twenty-One

Vera was shaking.

Joey stood by her side, ensuring her safety every step of the way. She was in the dining room and doing what she loved to do – serving Tyler's guests.

Every man was focused on food, and not worrying about anything else. Little did they know what was going on upstairs.

When Tyler explained what he had planned, Vera was horrified. Her concern lay in the fact the lawmen, guards, or Tyler could be injured, or worse, killed. She knew exactly what Horace was capable of.

She'd been lucky. His bullet only grazed her, but had it not been for Tyler rescuing her, Vera would not be alive today. Or she would be working in a brothel with no chance of a normal life.

Vera leaned into Joey. "I'm scared," she whispered.

Joey glanced down into her face. "I know," he said. "I am too. With Tyler at the helm, it will be fine. You will be fine."

She glared at him. "It's not me I'm worried about," she said in a huff, then strolled over to the beautifully set table. "More wine?" she asked one of the guests.

The man stared up at her and smiled. "Thank you, yes. You're new here," he said moments before his eyes focused on her gold wedding ring. "Who's the lucky man?" he asked loudly, then glanced over his shoulder at Joey.

"Not me," Joey said. "Vera is Tyler's wife."

The guest appeared deflated, but Vera handled it. She was used to flirty customers. "I'm so sorry," she said. "We should have met sooner."

The guest laughed, and the others joined in.

Without warning, silence filled the room. Vera glanced up to see Tyler standing in the doorway. He didn't look at all disheveled, nor did he appear worried. "Got them," he said firmly, then greeted his guests.

Vera thought she would collapse in relief. Before it could happen, Tyler came to her side and held her in his arms.

She had never felt so cosseted in all her life.

Joey cleared his throat, causing Vera to glance up. He grinned at her, and she smiled. Joey had become very special to her, and Vera knew he would always be her friend. "I have to clear the table," she whispered to Tyler, but it was clear he didn't want to let her go.

It was then she understood how much she meant to him. She felt the same way, but as a waitress, she had a job to do.

She pulled out of her new husband's arms and began to clear the soiled dishes. She placed them on the food trolley, ready to place back in the dumbwaiter. Joey helped her to distribute the cherry cobbler, and they all stood back and watched the guests as they clearly enjoyed the meal.

"I don't know what went down tonight," one of the guests said, "but it's clear something did. Despite that, you have ensured we all had an excellent meal. As usual," he finished.

The others nodded their agreement.

Warmth filled Vera. This is where she wanted to live forever. As long as she was with Tyler and Joey. She had no real ties to Eden. It was merely a place she worked and lay her head. She was simply going through the motions day after day.

Here in Robinvale, it felt like home. Her friends were here, she now felt safe, and she was happy. Vera hoped it never changed.

~*~

The trial date had been expedited. Not only did the sheriff want Horace Dalton dealt with as a matter of urgency, so did the marshals, along with the county judge. The man had caused havoc wherever he went.

Jason Gawne was also on trial, but his charges were not so severe. The only charge against him was attempted kidnap only due to proof being limited. It could still mean life in prison if found guilty. Horace on the other hand would probably hang for his multiple crimes against humanity.

Vera sat nervously in the courtroom. She was not alone. Apart from Joey and Tyler, the unfortunate women Horace had abducted and made into slaves were also there. There were dozens of them, and it was clear they were grateful to have been released from Horace's evil clutches.

The proceedings went in a whirl. As the star witness, Vera had to repeat the details of her abduction, the fear Horace caused, and the terror she'd endured because of it.

Tyler helped her back to her seat, and Vera felt her nerves settle as a result.

The judge called the other victims up one by one for their statements. After only a handful of women had testified, he put a halt to the proceedings. "I have heard enough evidence," he said firmly. "I am ready to give my judgement.

Horace Dalton, you will never see the light of day again. Except to be hanged by your neck until you are dead." Judge Hodgkins waved for Horace to be removed from the courtroom. "Jason Gawne, unfortunately I cannot prove you to be complicit in the brothel or the multiple kidnaps. I do however have enough evidence you attempted to assist Horace Dalton in the kidnap of Vera Evans, so you will live out the rest of your life in jail. Hard labor," he added, then waved for the deputies to remove the second prisoner.

As much as the result was what they all hoped for, Vera felt sad for Jason. He was a relatively young man. How he'd become entangled with Horace and his vile business, they may never know.

He did, however, make the decision to do so, and to profit from the misery of others. Her heart fluttered knowing she never had to look over her shoulder again.

"To all their victims," the judge added, glancing across the room, "there is nothing I can't change what you've been through. The sheriff's office will work with you to provide compensation, which will help you get your lives back. That money will come from Horace's hefty bank account. We will do whatever we can to restore your former life."

The judge then pounded his gavel and stood. The proceedings were over, and they could now get on with their lives.

Vera breathed a sigh of relief. Her ordeal was over, and she could now get on with her life with Tyler.

Epilogue

One year later...

"I really wish you would sit down." Joey's voice, although gentle, was full of concern.

Tyler entered the kitchen and glanced about. He didn't ask the question – he didn't need to. Vera had clearly done far more than she should.

He had only agreed to her continuing to work in the kitchen with Joey because it made her happy. In her current state, he'd already been having second thoughts.

His wife was white as a ghost, and her hands were shaking. Food was abandoned on the kitchen counter, and Joey's face was full of concern. Tyler hurried to Vera's side and led her to a chair. It was then he saw it. The puddle that told him her water had broken.

"It's too early," she whispered. The two men stared down at her, neither one moving. "Get the doctor!"

she demanded. "Otherwise, you will be delivering this baby right here in the kitchen."

Tyler's brain seemed to click in then. He didn't know the first thing about delivering babies, and quite frankly, he wasn't prepared to learn.

"I'll get the doc, you stay here with Vera," Joey told him. Moments later he was gone.

Tyler stood by Vera's side until the doctor arrived. That's when the dilemma became clear. Neither of them wanted their baby to be born in the stark kitchen, but neither did they want to take the difficult trip up the stairs to one of the bedrooms.

Vera wanted to have her baby at home.

Tyler huddled with Joey and the doc. The only solution was to place her on a trolley – the sort the ambulance used – and get her home. It had only been a matter of weeks since their new home had been finished. Vera didn't want to bring up their family in a gambling hall, and frankly, Tyler did not blame her.

He did consider it at one point, but the renovations would have been long and costly, and neither of them felt it appropriate. Instead, they compromised and built a home on the outskirts of town. It sat on two acres of land, had a small vegetable garden, a barn for their horses, and a paddock for the horses to run in.

It might have been close to town, but it was their very own patch of heaven. Tyler could already imagine their children running around the property when they were older. He could see them riding the horses, and more than anything, he could see the love he and Vera would give their family.

An almighty scream from Vera brought him back to the present. "Almost home," he told her gently. As he unlocked the door, Tyler held her hand. They went inside, and it wasn't long until the doc kicked him and Joey out.

His nurse arrived soon afterwards.

What seemed like hours later, Tyler was summoned back inside to meet his newborn son, Joseph.

Joey was by Tyler's side and was immediately declared the baby's godfather. They both stared down into Joseph's face, their own features softening.

"Thank goodness he looks like Vera," Joey said jokingly. Tyler jabbed him in the ribs. After all they'd been through together, after everything that happened, they were still the best of friends.

Tyler went to his wife's side and hugged her. "Thank you for our beautiful boy," he said, his voice full of emotion.

In that moment, Tyler knew despite everything she'd endured, if it hadn't been for Horace Dalton, he would never have met Vera. He also knew he would not be the happy man he was now.

If only they'd met decades ago… Despite that, Tyler knew they would spend the rest of their lives together. And God willing, their family would continue to grow.

From the Author

Thank you so much for reading my book – I hope you enjoyed it.

I would greatly appreciate you leaving a review where you purchased, even if it is only a one-liner. It helps to have my books more visible!

~*~

About the Author

Multi-published, award-winning and bestselling author Cheryl Wright, former secretary, debt collector, account manager, writing coach, and shopping tour hostess, loves reading.

She writes historical romantic suspense and historical western romance.

She lives in Melbourne, Australia, and is married with two adult children, six grandchildren, and three great-grandchildren.

When she's not writing, she can be found in her craft room making greeting cards.

Links

Website: http://www.cheryl-wright.com/

Facebook Reader Group:

https://www.facebook.com/groups/cherylwrightaut
hor/

Join My Newsletter:

https://cheryl-wright.com/newsletter/
(and receive a free book)